INVITATION TO DEATH

"Welcome," said the cold voice dripping with lies and deceit. "I've been expecting you."

Ted Rockson focused on the man who sat in the misty dimness at the far end of the room behind a long wooden desk, his thin pale hands clasped together on the heavily waxed top. It was Killov. The Skull. And he was unarmed.

"Thanks for the greeting," Rockson said, his shot-pistol pointed at the man's chest. "But you're going to come as a prisoner to stand trial for war crimes—or die right now. However you want it!"

"Tsk, tsk," Killov said. "You should be taught some manners. Pity you won't get a chance to learn."

The Blackshirt leader jerked his knee up under the desk, pressing a button. There was a roar from the front of Killov's desk as the wooden panels flew off and a mounted rack of ten shotguns simultaneously discharged a wall of waist-high shot at the Doomsday Warrior . . .

DOOMSDAY WARRIOR

#8 AMERICAN GLORY

BY RYDER STACY

ZEBRA BOOKS
KENSINGTON PUBLISHING CORP.

ZEBRA BOOKS

are published by

Kensington Publishing Corp.
475 Park Avenue South
New York, NY 10016

First printing: April 1986

Printed in the United States of America

Chapter One

Picture a paradise. Picture a field filled with flowers of every hue, stretching off to all the horizons waving, dancing in the wind like beckoning fingers of purest utopia. Picture petals on these rainbow flowers as soft as silk, with rivers of molten gold streaming through their spider-web veins. Picture fruits hanging from soft bending trees, branches reaching down to deliver their luscious cargo so human arms needn't reach, legs needn't stretch. Picture pink and orange and blue and green fruits in myriad shapes and sizes, bursting with juices and pulpy thick flesh. Picture birds with peacock tails hanging down below them from their high perches, their wings filled with luminescent feathers so subtle and rich that a Michaelangelo could spend a century cataloguing their tones. Picture parrots and hummingbirds and saucer-eyed owls, all cooing and chirping out their melodious ode to existence in a constant chorus that echoes through the moist, pungent groves of trees that fill the field. Picture a paradise.

Look closer in this picture of paradise. Peer deep into the rainbow. Pry apart the bands of color and peer beneath the purples, the oranges, the globes of sweet fruit like a woman's hot breasts. Peer closer beneath the feathers, beneath the silky petals. See the teeth, the claws that hide waiting to snatch anything that ventures near. See the hooked rows of daggers hidden in the hummingbird's throat, the digestive juices of steaming acid that line the bowels of the daisies nodding happily in the noonday sun. The thorns of the rose bush as sharp as razors and dripping with a poison that could take out the nervous system of an elephant like an ICBM missile shot straight from the underworld. Picture a paradise that is a living hell.

"Oh, look, Rock, how beautiful," Kim Langford said, pointing from her position atop her hybrid horse which rocked its hips back and forth lazily as it moved at a slow, even gait across the prairie. 'Brids knew — better than any creature alive, perhaps — that the longest journey was made one slow step at a time, and they carried out that knowledge with a thoroughly lazy vengeance.

Ted Rockson shifted slightly in his saddle, trying to make his aching thigh muscles a little more comfortable. He sighted in the direction that Kim was pointing. A field — filled with trees and flowers and fruits. A veritable oasis out here in the middle of nowhere. Nice. Maybe too nice.

"Oh, can we?" the blond daughter of Charles Langford, the newly elected president of the Re-United States of America who rode just paces ahead of them, asked in an excited voice. "It's been days

6

since we've had rest or seen anything worth seeing other than this sand filled with nothing but wart-faced lizards and cacti." Rock, Kim, her father, and a squad of Freefighters from Century City had been on the move for nearly two weeks now, traveling as many hours a day as Rock felt they and the 'brids could stand. Their attack on the Octagon in Washington, D.C. had freed President Langford and Kim from the KGB. Snatched right from under the nose of Colonel Killov, the psychotic leader of the Blackshirts. Rock knew that the man would not take kindly to said occurrence. And he didn't want to face an armada of attack choppers without an inch of cover for a hundred miles. Not with the president of the U.S., the first elected leader in more than a hundred years, and his daughter, the woman Rockson loved, in his charge. Rock's own death would be of no great loss — at least to him. But theirs would be a disaster for every citizen, every slaveworker, every Freefighter in America. There was too much at stake to slacken for even a second.

"I don't think we should, Kim," Rock said slowly, knowing as he spoke that she wasn't going to go for it. "I never much trusted things that pop up out of nowhere, things that shouldn't quite be where they are. 'Cause there's usually a reason — and it's usually bad."

"Oh, Rock, you're so paranoid sometimes," Kim snapped at him, her already alabaster cheeks growing a whiter shade. "We're safe by now. They would have caught up to us days ago. We're out of chopper range — at least from D.C. Come on," she said, growing softer. "Please. We don't have to stay long.

7

Just gather some fruits, let the 'brids drink. I think I see a pond ahead," she said, smiling with the sudden enthusiasm of a child whose face can go from anger to pure delight in a second, in the passing of a cloud. Perhaps that was why he loved her, Rockson thought, and his heart filled with an inexpressible mixture of longing and pain at her sudden perfect beauty as she smiled at him, unveiled, unarmored. While he, the warrior who had fought for so many years he had long since stopped counting the number of dead, the lakes of blood, the skies of smoke and the stench of mass death . . . he had almost become dried up inside, so filled with the despair of mankind, that only a deep and darkly humorous cynicism fueled him and kept him going into yet more battles. Until her. Until how she looked right now.

"Yeah, sure," the Doomsday Warrior said, so softly she could hardly hear him. Though he knew in his guts it wasn't right, he said, "Sure, let's go." But slowly, unconsciously, he released the safety on the .12 gauge death dealer that sat at his side, waiting.

Kim whipped the reins quickly from side to side on her 'brid's shoulder and the shaggy creature stubbornly added a few steps to its stride. The closer she got, the less Kim could believe her eyes. It wasn't just a field—it was—it was—like the Bible. The word snapped into her head. The Bible—like Adam and Eve. Fruits, dripping with a sappy dew, hung everywhere ready to burst their luscious innards out onto the world. Flowers like crazy quilts sewn from all the colors of the spectrum surrounded her, filling her eyes with a kaleidoscope of petals and leaves. Even the 'brid seemed to grow excited by the presence of so much beauty and rocked its back legs in the air, bucking around like a rodeo bronco. Kim tried to hold on but was tossed into the air, landing on her rump in a thick growth of purple lilacs as deeply violet as a king's royal robe. They cushioned her fall like a bed of the softest fingers on earth and her nostrils filled with the overpowering perfumes.

Rockson rode up, pulling his 'brid to a skidding stop, and jumped down to her. "Are you all right?" he asked, his mismatched violet and aquamarine eyes burning with a tense fire.

"Oh, Rock, it's—it's beautiful," she laughed up at him, stretching her arms for the Doomsday Warrior to come to her. Her eyes were moist and wide and Rockson couldn't resist. His face widened into a broad grin and he dropped to his knees, falling on top of her. He held her as tightly as he had ever held a woman in his life. And she pressed her small firm breasts up against him, flattening them against his chest until she was almost one with him. And just for a second they looked into each other's eyes, totally open, telepathic in love, their souls flying back and forth like wisps of silver fog. This might be the most perfect moment in their lives. Here and then gone as such things are, in a meteoric flash, burned up by the atmosphere of reality. They tried to file the feeling away in the center of their hearts before it disappeared. Then it was gone. Rockson realized that Kim's father would be just behind them with the rest of the Freefighters and it would hardly do for the president of the United States to find his daughter in the bushes with the military commander of Century City. Rock sighed and pulled himself away from Kim, with a deep sadness passing across his eyes like green strontium clouds flying high across the face of the moon.

"Will you look at this," Detroit Green coughed, jumping down from his 'brid before it could come to a complete stop. The black Freefighter landed amidst a hillock of dandelions and he began dancing through them, sending the fuzzy little balls of white fibers into the air like a snowstorm of feathers. The others dismounted, their tough battle-hardened faces taking on face-cracking smiles as they were, to a man, unable to resist being moved by the impossible lushness and color of the oasis. They wandered through patches of yellow and red, taking off their boots and letting the velvet tongues of vegetation run across their calloused toes like silk scarves dangled by a courtesan. Their faces seemed to uncoil like a steel spring that has been wound up so tightly that the very fibers of its metal being seem ready to pop. Then release—their muscles loosened, their eyes grew wider and wider in fascination at the fantastic surroundings. And like little boys in a dream, a dream of a world they had never known before but only seen in books and movies of the old days, they wandered around in a daze of aesthetic intoxication.

Balboni was the first to scream. All ears turned to track the source of the howling—then they saw him. He had bent down to inhale the sweet aroma of an immense pink-petaled plant with dayglow green dots covering it like a chlorophyll leopard. He had pushed his face right up into the soft petals, had rubbed his cheeks against the smoothest thing he had ever felt.

Suddenly petals were closing around him, engulfing his head. Their softness turned hard as tiny spikes eased out of the petals, grabbing hold of his skull and undulating as they began pulling his entire body slowly, inexorably into the caustic digestive acids of the flesh-eating stomach hidden in its roots below the ground.

The paradise turned into hell. The flowers amidst which the Freefighters lay reached for them—tendrils suddenly clawed, spiked leaves slashed madly at them, vines snaked around the 'brids' legs, pulling at them. Hook-beaked owls swooped down from their perches, their faces not cute any longer but hideous, terrifying—with rows of angled razor teeth snapping at the struggling human prey.

"Jesus Christ," Rockson muttered as he rose to his feet, pulling Kim up with him in a flash. They were being attacked on every side. The peaceful meadow had erupted into a violent twisting and snapping in which every living thing was trying to get them. Every leaf, every petal, every branch, every piece of dripping fruit was lunging madly at the humans who had come near them. Before the Doomsday Warrior could take a step, he felt a snaking vine wind around his ankle and up his leg. The thing was brown like the underside of a log and dripping with a vile juice which was already eating small holes in the sides of Rockson's thick plastisynth field pants. His hand moving in a blur, Rockson whipped out his .12 gauge shotpistol and fired a load just inches from his boot into the writhing vegetable snake's body. It exploded in a thick noxious spray of brown and the tendril around his leg dropped to the ground like a piece of rotting garbage. At least the damned things were mortal, Rockson thought, letting a quick whistle of thanks pass through his teeth.

"Use your weapons!" the Doomsday Warrior screamed out over the bray of yelling men and howling hybrids and snapping birds of every size and shape who flew down from the nearby trees in an invasion of murderous beaks and talons. "Your weapons, your weapons!" Rockson screamed again, running forward, firing at twisting bouquets of roses that snapped out with poisoned thorns and patches of carnivorous sunflowers, whose huge white and yellow petaled heads leaned far forward, spitting out a spray of disabling mist. One of the 'brids went down and was instantly covered in a thousand little arms of green and black vines, its body literally ripped apart, as each tendril dug into the hot flesh with snapping pincers.

But Rockson's thunderous shots had at least snapped the rest of the team from their mesmerized flailings at their would-be killers. The men reached for their pistols, knives, anything they were carrying and unleashed their own human version of death. Stalks and shoots, tendrils and stamens exploded into a greenish brown slime that filled the air with an acrid mist. Somehow, most of the men broke free of their captors, grabbed their 'brids, and rushed toward Rockson, who had gone over to Balboni. The Freefighter's head had disappeared into the spotted leaves of the huge meateater, right up to the shoulders. At least he was still alive, Rock could see instantly by the pushing of Balboni's hands against the outer petals as the man tried to break free. Rockson didn't even try to pry off the sucking yard-long petals, for they were closed as tight as a Venus fly-trap over an insect. Instead the Doomsday Warrior knelt down and aimed the big muzzle of his .12 gauge right at the spot where the carnivorous roots entered the dirt. He turned his head and pulled the trigger. The foot-thick stem shattered as if cut down by a scythe, the black pulp oozing down into the dirt. The huge stalk and the petals holding Balboni captive fell over and the Freefighter toppled to the ground, still stuck inside.

Rock reached over with his hunting blade and sliced carefully around the neck and face of the captive, working his knife as if he were skinning a deer. But with the death of its circulatory system, the plant quickly released its hold and the speckled flowers fell open and limply down, already losing their shape and color.

Rockson had to turn away for a second, as he saw the freed man. Balboni was a mess. The plant's inner jaws and digestive fluids had begun to work on the prey. The entire outer layer of flesh had been eaten away, dissolved like a melting bubble. The acid had chewed away all of the Freefighter's hair, his eyebrows, lips, and ears. Parts of the subdermal system below had been melted into view, and one could clearly see the entire anatomical structure of the musculature of the throat and face as if displayed on a medical school mannikin.

"R-r-oock," a voice somehow managed to utter from between fleshless lips. "It — got me. The fucker g-g-got meee." With that Balboni twitched slightly just once and fell still as stone to the blood- and vegetable-spattered soil. Rockson cradled the man's head, slowly lowering it, setting it softly on its final cushion on the grass. Balboni was lucky he was dead, Rock thought. He wouldn't have wanted to live looking like that. The plant must have injected some sort of poison into the bloodstream—like a spider—to hold and keep its much larger prey.

But there wasn't time for deep meditations—not when the landscape was trying to eat his entire force, including the president of the United States. Rockson shot to his feet as the others gathered around him, firing every second, reloading and firing again. They bunched together in an ever-tighter circle, grabbing at the reins of their hybrids who stomped and neighed out furious bellowings of fear. Rockson could see that the entire defensive formation was about to crack under the relentless pressure of the attacking plant and bird life which came at them from every side. He saw a sudden large shadow swooping down and fired straight up in the air. Something burst just yards above him and bloody feathers floated down onto his head and shoulders.

Suddenly he remembered an ancient U.S. Army training film on mine clearing—field-style—that he'd seen back in Century City. A vine slithered in, trying to hook his foot, but Rockson pulled the foot away and brought it down hard on the reaching petals, squashing them into pulp with his steel-heeled boots. There was no more time.

"Archer, Chen, Detroit!" Rock screamed out. "Front and center." The Chinese-American martial arts expert rushed through the frantically firing Freefighters with Archer, the seven-foot half-mute mountain man, and Detroit, the ebony-skinned grenade expert of the squad, right behind him.

"Get out your stuff, boys," the Doomsday Warrior said, pointing back toward the way they'd come in. "We'll have to blast our way through. Chen—some of your exploding star knives, spin them out every ten feet or so! Archer—your phosphorus arrows. You understand me?" he asked, looking closely into the huge fighter's eyes as the mountain man was not always 100% in the analysis department. But this time, the barn door of a Freefighter understood perfectly.

"Buuurrrn 'eem, Rooooocck," he said, whipping an arrow into the slot of his wide steel-wire crossbow.

"Detroit—your magnesium grenades—heave 'em up fifty feet or so. You'll be our long-range artillery—so you're going to have to take out a lot of 'em!"

"It's barbecue time, Rock," the short but ripplingly muscular black fighter spat, ripping two grenades from the twin belts across his barrel chest.

"Go! Go!" the Doomsday Warrior yelled out as the three men took the lead of the panic-stricken group. Rockson glanced around to make sure Kim and her father were all right and saw them, completely surrounded by his men in the center of the defensive concentration. They were as safe as they were going to be.

Detroit pulled the pins from his two pineapples and heaved first his right then his left arm straight ahead. The two balls of super-concentrated high explosives soared through the air like the throw of a left fielder trying to cut off the runner at home. They hit the ground and lay there for a second or two as if they

15

were duds. Then they both went off simultaneously, sending up a cloud of steaming plant life in steaming geysers.

The team took off, the men pulling their circle in at the flanks so they became a moving wedge, protected on each flank by the 'brids, which were stronger and better able to break free of the constant entangling tendrils of the field's murderous plant life. Detroit pulled another two grenades and threw them about fifty feet ahead of the first while Archer released an arrow to the right where an entire tree was holding its long spiked branches out and waving them at the fleeing Freedomfighters, trying to snatch something, anything. The arrow buried itself in the thing's trunk just feet above the ground and burst into a white-hot flame, roaring instantly with a furnace-like whistle. The flames must have sent some sort of message to the thing's primitive nervous system, as it reared back and emitted a high-pitched scream that the men couldn't hear—but the hybrids reacted to it with alarm, rising up on their hind legs and windmilling their front hooves at the air as if fighting off an invisible enemy. The flaming tree pulled back, its very roots lifting up out of the ground as it rushed through the field—a blazing bonfire.

Chen kept an eye on the closer of the plant attackers, taking the very lead of the wedge. His almond eyes scanned the growth in front of them, waiting to sense the tiniest movement. There—to the left, 15 feet ahead. He flipped one of the five-pointed throwing knives and caught the base of a clump of beetle-jawed spider plants. A thousand green legs shot off in every direction, severed by the quite

16

powerful explosion of the small device. A swarm of hook-beaked crows with shining purple-black feathers came soaring down from above, a good two dozen of them. They emitted caws of hunger as they extended their three-inch-long talons, their reptilian eyes sighting fresh meat. Two of Chen's whizzing saw blades came up to greet them, sending out a blast that ripped wings from bodies, plucking the murderous flock's feathers from their very sides. Half-cleaned birds dropped down onto the fleeing Freefighters, ready for the oven. A branch from a willow tree reached over and tried to grab hold of the Chinese destroyer, but Chen treated it as he would any other opponent. He sidestepped the snapping thick-barked branch and lashed out a sidekick. Twelve feet of the branch cracked and fell to the ground, bleeding a thick green fluid with a swampy odor.

As if suddenly alarmed that they were about to lose their meal tickets, the plant life, the flowers, the spiked groundhogs all closed in with renewed fury. But the humans fought back just as savagely, every man in the unit firing away at anything that came near him. Leaving a trail of green and brown slime behind them, the Freefighters somehow blasted their way back to the edge of the prairie. With the last man out on the soil where the plants couldn't reach, Rockson turned and looked back. A hybrid had been caught and tripped by a grove of giant hyacinths, their tiny teeth tearing away at the poor thing's stomach and chest. But everyone else seemed safe. Kim rushed over to Rockson and leaned against him, wanting to feel his strength in her moment of terror.

"*You* were right, Rock," she said softly. "I was

wrong. And a man died because of it." Her eyes began glistening with moisture.

"There's no time for tears," the Doomsday Warrior said, cupping her chin and kissing her lightly on the lips. "Every man here could be dead at any moment. We all know that. Many have died. Many more will die. And many of them have died because of orders I gave—and will give again. It's a war, Kim. Men . . . and women . . . die in wars. So—no tears. None of us has the luxury of guilt."

Rockson said a few words of prayer as the Freefighters stood around him, just yards away from the edge of the field whose occupants continued to writhe around in a fury of displeasure. Rock couldn't see Balboni's body from his vantage point. But if there was anyone up there listening—he would know who they were talking about.

"Take this man,
Into your world
And know that he was a brave fighter
Who gave his life so that others might be free.
And tell the bastard we'll miss him."

The Freefighters mounted their still-skittish hybrids, whose nervous mouths were filled with a bubbling yellow foam of pure fear. They were happy as hell to be away from the cursed place and took off at a gallop as Rockson veered the force off to the right. They'd have to circumnavigate the deathfield. It would take them perhaps a hundred miles out of their way back to Century City. But there was no option. Not with a jungle trying to kill them at every step. Within minutes the killer plants were just a bad, bad memory in every man's mind.

Balboni's body lay there, the hands twitching slightly from the nerve-contracting effects of the poison that the plant, which had half-digested his face, had injected into him. That plant was dead now, in pieces around its intended victim, blasted apart by Rockson's shotpistol. But others lived. Others were hungry. From beneath his back, the green grass began shooting up like spikes protruding from an iron maiden. They entered the flesh all along his spinal cord and sank their razor-edged suction cups into the arteries along his backbone. The green jaws poked long curved drinking spears into the still-pumping bloodstream. And they drank, sucking the slowly cooling blood into their root systems. A thousand vampires fed on the Freefighter's body until there wasn't a drop left to drink. Then the vines closed in for the flesh.

Chapter Two

"Pow, right in the—?" a hidden voice screamed down from high in a fir tree.

"Kisser," Rock yelled up. "It's all right, boys, it's just me, Rockson, and a few of my friends. Thought we'd stop in here for a little brunch." The thick needled branches of the tree parted twenty-five feet up. First a rifle barrel, then a face poked through.

"Damn, it *is* Rockson. Didn't know where the hell you'd gone off to this time. It's all right, boys," the sentry shouted off at the other trees. A dozen rifles lowered, a dozen Freefighter guards relaxed and eased back down on their wooden plank stations.

"Well, just head on in," the guard yelled down. "They're using the Western 'Brid Tunnel now for the main entrance. Still ain't got the old one cleared. Maybe never will. You take care now."

Rockson led his party past the towering trees and along a narrow path that the hybrid horses tried to gallop down, having to be restrained by their riders. They knew they were home—rest, food, and whatever other mammalian dreams the strong-footed creatures held treasured in their brains. Rockson glanced around at the work crews still patching up the exterior of the mountain beneath which Century City lay. The neutron bomb dropped by Colonel Killov's air force had nearly decimated the subterranean world, destroying almost a third of its facilities, including its hydroponics level, hospital, archives, and some manufacturing sectors. Thousands of its citizens had been lost or severely wounded. But Century City had been born out of a disaster much worse than this—the nuke war of a hundred years earlier. Like the phoenix, she would rise from the ashes again and again—until there were no more ashes to rise from.

Still, it gave Rockson pause to see just how much the city he had lived in for years had changed. As they rode up to the entranceway to the mountain, several of the camouflaged guards recognized him and came running down to greet the Doomsday Warrior and the others in the party.

"Who're your friends, Rock?" asked Patterson, Jr., a freckle-faced teen with two front teeth missing from a recent run-in with a party of Reds, pointing to the somewhat bedraggled and tired-looking Langford and Kim, who was riding alongside trying to ease his discomfort. While in captivity in the Octagon in Washington, Killov's psychotic goons had had a little fun with Langford. And though none of it had caused permanent injury, still, his mind was in a state of semi-shock from the experience. He wore a dazed look on his face as if trying to remember some long-forgotten event.

"That's the president of this country," Rockson said with some pride. "Goddamned guy's been through hell and back over the last few years. Tougher than

22

me — by a long shot."

"He don't look too good," the teen said, with the honesty only those who don't know any better can spit out.

Rockson put his finger over his lips, not wanting Langford or Kim to hear. "Quiet," Rock whispered brusquely. "He'll be all right. You'd be hanging off your saddle if you'd just made the journey he did. So, get back up in your post and do a decent day's work out here, you hear me, boy?"

"Yes, sir," the youth said, his face nearly draining of blood. To be reprimanded by Ted Rockson was not his idea of the best way to start a day. He rushed back up to his station and with the help of another guard on the other side of the camouflaged entrance, the two of them pulled on long cables and slowly the thick netting slid aside.

Rockson rode through into the dimly lit chamber, glaring up once again at the offending guard. He knew why he'd gotten so angry, though. Because it was true. The president *did* look like shit. No one was saying it. Everyone, especially Kim, was acting as though things were just fine. But Rock knew the look. Perhaps Langford's body was all right. But in his eyes — and consequently in the brain behind them — something had gone out. Some fire that had fueled the man all these years. Years of trekking back and forth across America, trying to rouse its populace, trying to restore the democratic ways of old. And it had worked — for Langford had become the most well-known man among the non-slave American citizens in their hidden cities, in their farms far from the reach of Russian patrols. Like Ted Rockson,

Langford was a legend. And in the Re-Constitutional Convention held just months before, which delegates from all the free cities had attended, Langford had won by a landslide—the first freely elected American president for a hundred years.

And now . . . Rock couldn't bear to look the man right in the eyes, to see the signs of defeat, of old age, creeping in. It wasn't his fault. How much can a man take? How much pressure can his heart, his veins stand? How many thoughts and fears and paranoias and crushed dreams can his brain withstand before it crumbles like a wall beneath the grinding tides of life? Rock silently prayed that the man would fight his way back once more. For they needed him. Every man and woman in America needed him. The symbolism of a president—a leader, a spiritual and moral guide, was a thousand times more powerful than the biggest mortar shell, the most destructive anti-tank cannon.

The work teams were still bustling along the blasted rock tunnel that Rockson and the expedition-ary force slowly moved down atop their whinnying 'brids, which were growing more and more impatient by the second for the warmth and safety of their corrals. The amount of work accomplished in the few weeks Rockson had made his cross-country foray to snatch the president was amazing. Nearly all the rubble that had littered the inside of the Freefighting city had been cleared. Much of the power had been restored, and emergency lights had been strung up along the thoroughfares that had been used previ-ously as secondary routes but were now bustling highways. Men and women pushed and pulled dollies and wagons filled with everything from freshly hewn rock to be dumped into the bottomless chasm at the northern side of the city to crates of Liberator rifles — still being turned out, albeit at about half their pre-nuke-hit rate. But Century City's main industry — the production of the automatic 9mm rifle — could not stop. For it was these weapons, shipped out by pack team across the length and breadth of America, that were the guerillas' main weapon against the Reds. Many of the smaller towns and villages which had managed to remain free often had only old shotguns or pistols in their armories. Thus, Century City, under the scientific and production tutelage of Dr. Shecter, had become the cornerstone for the rearming of America. Her work couldn't cease for a moment.

They came to the debriefing chamber where the party dismounted, the hybrids taken away by stableboys to be cleaned and fed. They all entered the side chamber where a taped voice told them to disrobe and go through the normal decontamination procedures. Rock told Kim to go across to the other side to the women's decon rooms. Then he disrobed, walked into one of a row of high plastisteel booths, stood in the middle, and closed his eyes. He had been through it so many times that now it was really just a nuisance — though he could remember back to the first days when Shecter had had them installed — and demanded that everyone go through them when they had been out of the city for more than 24 hours. The invigorating spray of soap and water that slapped into the flesh like a masseur's pounding hands. Then the ultrasound and the violet waves of light rippling down his body.

At last the speaker above him pinged, the door slid open with a whisper of air, and Rock stepped out and into the set of freshly laundered and pressed civvies — khaki slacks and shirt and deck sneakers that lay waiting for him, automatically deposited by conveyor belt on a low table next to the decon booth.

Rath was waiting, pencil in one hand, writing pad in the other, as usual. Century City's Intel chief was nothing if not enthusiastic about his job. Too enthusiastic, as far as Rockson was concerned. "Let's —," he began.

"Not right now," the Doomsday Warrior said, brushing past the man. "I'm just not in the mood."

"It's regulations, Rock. You know that. All incoming forces shall receive an initial debriefing of at least basic successes and failures of their missions. Military Manual — Section 4, Para —"

"Rath," Rockson said, slowing just slightly and looking the security chief square in the eyes. "I've just ridden more miles than a snarlizard has teeth. I've been shot, stabbed, blown up, bitten, spat on, punched, and things I can't even remember — but they still hurt. So not right now. If you need something to do — go talk to the president of the United States," Rock growled, pointing back toward the decon room. "And see that his daughter, Kim, gets first-class — and I *mean* first-class — treatment. Okay?"

"The president — you got him?" Rath asked, his eyes widening. Not a one of the council that had sent Rockson out on the rescue mission, Rath included, had really thought it was possible.

"Yeah, got him — and the man's got problems. So keep your people's noses out of his face and get the

26

medical and psych units on it right away." Rockson turned to head out to his room where all he wanted was a few hours of uninterrupted shuteye.

"One thing before you go," Rath said. "I've got to tell you that from our sources' accounts—which are admittedly often exaggerated—from around the country, Killov's Blackshirts have taken from 60% to 75% of the Red Army fortresses. There's an emergency meeting about the Soviet's little civil war—tonight, in three hours. Should I—"

"For Christ's sake, yeah, wake me," Rockson spat out, heading through the newly hung, slightly off-center door that led to the main thoroughfare. "Though I wish you hadn't told me until later. Even in my goddamned dreams I'll be worrying about what the hell to do next." He gave a grudging smile to Rath, who returned it, and then quickly headed off to find the president.

Rath slid the pencil back in his pocket and the pad behind and under his jacket. Even Rath understood that one did not go up to the president of the United States and start interrogating him like some corporal just back from shooting up a few Russian tricks. The Intel chief pulled out his best diplomatic smile and hung it like bright laundry across his countenance.

Rockson moved through the main square of Century City, looking around this way and that at the repairs that were taking place. Nearly the entire ceiling had been stabilized and some of the machinery of the smaller factories, if not their walls, had been pulled together. The whole underground city had the raw unpolished look of bare rock, since it was sculpted right out of the granite. It looked much as it must have when the original founders—those thousands of people in cars and buses and trucks inside the Interstate tunnel in Colorado—were trapped by the nearby detonation of a nuke. They had carved their home from the walls of the tunnel, burrowing right into the side of the rich iron-ore mountain for living and storage—and eventually science and hydroponics, along with all the myriad departments that now existed within the hidden mini-metropolis.

Rockson greeted all those who recognized him as they scurried past, waving, managing a smile. These were *his* people—the workers, the fighters. Not the top brass, not the decision makers, just men—men ready to rip down walls with their bare hands, or pick up a rifle and take on a Russian convoy. Men the Doomsday Warrior had been fighting next to for many years.

He walked along the rampways, since the elevator system was still largely nonfunctional except for medical needs and priority movement of equipment. He'd have to look around, see how the rebuilding was progressing—particularly up in Shecter's sci labs. But later. Everything later. At last he reached his room, thinking that it would perhaps be occupied by one of the wounded from the cave-in of the city. They had been commandeering rooms when he left. But he gingerly opened the door—and there was no one. It was just as he had left it. A bare concrete square with a bed, a mirror, a small plywood closet for his things. Not that he had many things, but the occasional oddity or object of beauty he found on one of his endless missions. A set of horns, a yard long and gnarled and curled into a complex weave of curved bone, poked out from one wall. It glowed a dim but piercing red, almost into the infrared spectrum. He had found it months before and couldn't resist its hypnotic beauty. Shecter's lab boys, who inspected everything that was brought in from the outside—be it fur or feather, rock or shell, and catalogued them in the city's rapidly expanding scientific computerized information center—couldn't figure out how the hell it gave off the glow it did, or how or why the animal who had possessed the horns had used them.

But Rockson didn't care why. The why's were for the smockcoats. For him, life was beyond explanation. It was a mystery that was handed to him in new ways and in new forms every day. And there was no choice except to take it—and try to stay alive.

Rock shut the door, not turning on the light. The red glow of the horns illuminated the room just enough to see. He disrobed again, folding the civilian clothes over the chair and then sat on the bed, kneeling cross-legged. He put the palms of his hands together in the cupping *mudra* and closed his eyes, breathing out deeply.

It took only minutes for him to fall into a deep meditative trance in which every system in his body had slowed to nearly a tenth its normal speed. His very cells relaxed, uncoiled in the ultra-breath meditation. He had not had even one second to relax the entire time they had been out hunting down the president. As the commander of the force, Rock could never rest. Never let down his guard, never even fully sleep, one eye open, the ears listening, always listening for the crack of a branch, the rustle of a leaf. And it took its toll. By the end of the journey he

29

felt wound tight as a spring, ready to pop, to explode, his brain filled with too many screams. But already it was disappearing into the windless void that he entered deep within himself.

He was nowhere. No one. His breath and the air of the world outside were the same. His cells were the cells of oxygen and hydrogen floating freely. He was just an idea. A concept of a thing, an energy organization that created the illusion of self.

He floated. Floated free. A sensation most men never feel. Only the birds and the fish know. No up or down, no gravity, just freedom, endless freedom to soar into nothing. He could feel his consciousness rise out of his body and float above him. He looked down and saw himself, the strong perfect physique of homo mutatiens — the new race — as evolved mentally and physically from homo sapiens as that species had been from the Neanderthals who they briefly shared the planet with. He could feel the strength of his body, the perfect motion of the heart and the arteries, the lungs and inner organs.

He soared higher, away from his body, through the molecules of the ceiling and through the floors above. He floated through the solid rock as if it were water, seeing it but somehow able to melt through its atoms. Rockson rose wingless, soaring into the night sky like a satellite of pure consciousness. Higher, into clouds and ethers, into magnetic rays. He glided along the gravity patterns that shot out and up from the poles of the earth, letting their pure energy push him along like a speck of dust in a tornado.

The Glowers had taught him. That hideous race of telepathic mutants with their entire nervous and muscular systems outside their bodies, the ugliest creatures perhaps that God had ever put on the face of the earth. But also, when one could join their mind-language — the gentlest and most beautiful. The Glowers had shown Rockson, using his latent mutant abilities, how to rise into the outer flesh of the planet — how to be one with it. Feel its heat waves, its tidal swells sweeping around the globe. Sense its gravity pulsations and its volcanic eruptions. They had shown him how to enter this world of unimaginable beauty and complexity. And he revelled in it. Flew like an eagle of pure consciousness among the oceans of atmosphere, absorbing their every hue, their every shadow of hidden spectral energies.

He heard them. Far off at first, like the howling of a storm wind through a distant forest. Then closer, singing, many minds joined, speaking as one, all thoughts joining, blending into a symphony of sensation, thought, smell, taste, touch. All in one. They sang to him.

"Rockson, we reach out to you once more. We warn you of terrible danger."

"Are you here, are you coming?" The Doomsday Warrior spoke out with his mind as he floated, spinning like an invisible meteor high above the curving surface of the cobalt blue earth below.

"No, we are at our camp. Where we taught you. The journey we made to help you at Forrester Valley, where we turned wishes to nightmares in the minds of the invading Nazi army — took something from us. The steering of the sandships, the leaving of our

31

poisoned radioactive zone—it weakened us. We cannot come again to help you with our powers. Not for a long time, perhaps never. We will help you with our minds, Rockson, but not our physicality."

"Yes," the Doomsday Warrior answered back with sadness, which he knew they would feel. For they sensed the emotion attached to all thoughts, all words.

"There is great danger. Perhaps greater than ever before. Killov, the skull, is moving faster than we thought possible. He has taken control of nearly all of Premier Vassily's and President Zhabnov's forces and fortresses here in our land. Killov is a sick, diseased person. To a depth and with a power that even you—who have done battle with him—cannot understand. He seeks to—destroy the world—utterly and completely."

They sent out a mental picture that slammed Rockson, pure energy though he was, and sent him spinning. A vision of Killov setting off all the nuclear missiles that were left. Aiming them at every portion of the world. They showed him the bombs going off. The thousand mushroom clouds—and then—the entire planet bursting apart at the seams like a rotten bag whose garbage had dropped out the bottom. Pieces the size of whole nations and fragments just blocks long flew out to every corner of the universe, rushing off to all the disparate galaxies that spun like wheels in the infinite night. Then—there was nothing. Where the earth had hung suspended in infinity—was now an emptiness. Not even an asteroid belt remained as the tombstone of the once-proud planet. Just black space, an unholy void, through which the sun burned with atomic rage.

Rockson felt a deep swelling inside his heart, which was far below. And the desire to cry, though he had no tears or eyes from which to weep.

"This, then, is the fate of the home of all of us, Rockson. American and Russian alike. Human, animal, all will perish if—" They left the thought unsaid. The collective mind stopped, not wanting to face the next, inevitable thought even themselves.

"Unless—" Rockson sent back.

"The future is very dark, like the sky before a tornado. The waves of fate itself are broken, crashing from different dimensions. We do not know the future. Can only sense it. We sense darkness, Rockson. A bottomless burning darkness. You must—fight this with everything you possess—and more."

Suddenly they pulled back, snatching their collective mind from telepathic contact with him with the speed of a missile flying off.

Rockson felt almost in a state of shock. His consciousness reeled from the nightmare vision of the total annihilation of earth. He felt himself losing his center, his cohesiveness, and strained to come down from the atmosphere. It was so hard. Things were tearing at him. Rays, forces beyond his comprehension all pulling at his mind, his soul. Somehow he shot down, down from the high ethers through the thick plutonium-tinged clouds, moving by instinctive connection back toward his body in suspension below. He found Century City and shot down through the ground, the concrete, slipping once again between the molecules. There it was—he—his body, almost silent, heart slowed to four beats a minute. Rockson

33

gathered his diffused mental being together and entered the skull, the heart, the spine of himself.

He was back. Inside his body. The burden of its flesh, the sensation of its hard bones and pumping blood was like suddenly carrying hundred-pound weights on each shoulder, each leg. It was painful, returning to the body. But the other way of being was too powerful—too explosive for him to handle for long. The Glowers were mutants in more than just a physical sense—they had to be, to live all their lives in that linked supra-human mode of macrocosmic consciousness. He could barely stand it for five minutes.

He came out of the meditation posture and fell backward on the bed, exhausted to the very marrow of his bones. He was asleep before he had the chance to wonder if he would be able to fall asleep.

Chapter Three

Colonel Killov, known simply to those who feared and hated him as "The Skull," tore through the luggage that stood just inside the front door of his six-room suite, searching frantically.

"Where are they? Where the fucking hell are they? Someone's going to die tonight. Do you hear me?" he screamed out to six KGB officers who stood nearby, staring straight down at the Persian rug on the floor.

"My medicines, my goddamned medicines. Where are they?" He ripped open suitcases, his skinny pale arms endowed with the strength of a maniac, and threw their contents through the air. Killov's dependence on various drugs over the years had reached the stage of drug addiction. Killov wasn't addicted to just one or even two drugs, but over a dozen. Not to mention the various ups, downs, and consciousness-expanding and consciousness-contracting vials, spansules, and capsules that he carried everywhere he traveled in a special manganese-plated suitcase.

But it was nowhere to be found. Somewhere in transit from Washington, D.C. — where KGB troops had been driven out by the onslaught of Rockson and his men, to Fort Minsk, where Killov had flown to oversee his ongoing military takeover of Red America—his suitcase had been lost. The war, the battles, the lives of hundreds of thousands of men were all secondary.

"Fools," Killov screamed, throwing the last of the suitcases down on the floor and kicking it a few yards to the KGB officers. "Why are you just standing there staring at me? Get my physician on the radio, call Denver, call the Monolith. There's always a full supply ready at the chemist's. Have it flown here—priority one. Do you hear me?" He came at them, flailing at their broad black-leathered chests with pale vein-popping hands. The officers fled as if a grizzly was after them. For as high-ranking as they were, they knew he would have them disposed of in a second if it suited his wishes—or his madness.

Killov sank to the floor and pushed the door closed behind him. Not one. Not one pill. He patted the pockets of his light-absorbing midnight-black field jacket, knowing the gesture was futile. They had all been in the suitcase, and now . . . whatever fool was responsible would pay. Would pay, oh yes. The colonel, the Supreme Leader of the Supreme Torturers of America, rose to his knees and raised one trembling, skeletal hand, flicking off the overhead light. There—at least he was in darkness. The dimness soothed him, cascading down around his gaunt face and shoulders like a shadowy blanket. Killov closed his eyes and tried to entice his mind with thoughts of the torture he would inflict on the guilty party. How he would slide the lips from his face, pour drops of acid onto his eyes, his tongue.

36

A stab of pain shot through his thigh as if someone had stabbed him, wrenching his mind back to his own pitiful state. He hadn't been without drugs for—how long had it been? Years. *Years.* He reached back into his memory, something he rarely did, but could see nothing. It felt as if he had always been this way. Had he had a childhood, a mother? Somewhere, shadows roamed—but out of reach.

His stomach suddenly contracted, squeezing his intestines like the closing grip of a steel vise as the withdrawal symptoms hit him. The KGB commander screamed out a hoarse croaking sound and fell forward on his face onto the ultra-lush intricately patterned rug. His brain felt as if it was on fire. An immense burning coal in the center of his cracking skull. Every muscle was filled with smoking mercury, sizzling his veins, scalding his arteries. His entire body spasmed like a snake and a thick yellow sputum erupted from his mouth, depositing itself in a putrid puddle on the rug.

He groaned and trembled, rolled around on the exotic carpet of the late commander of Fort Minsk. He was pure animal now. The sadist, the murderer, the madman with plans for world domination—and destruction—were all gone. Now just a creature, a puny amoeba undulating in wild pain. How long it went on, Killov had no idea. Just his own mind—and the moon, the razor fragments of its rays slicing through the uncovered window at the far side of the room, cutting into him with cruel neon waves that made him vomit again and again until there was nothing left inside, not a drop of moisture to retch.

A knock sounded at the door, hesitant at first, then

slightly louder.

"Yes, yes, come in," Killov barely managed to whisper through parched lips. The door opened and lights were flicked on and he threw his hands over his eyes to shield them from the lacerating rays. A hand was holding his head up, feeding pills into his mouth, then water. Killov gulped and swallowed, exploding again in a spraying cough. But he was able to keep the precious pills down. Slowly he opened his pinholes of eyes and brought the figure above him into focus. It was his personal physician, Keserensky, doing his best to look confident and smile down at the filth-encrusted shriveled creature he held in his arms.

"More," Killov burped out. "More pills. Codeine, Alevil, Transmorph." The obese physician, his jowls pushing out around his stiff collar and hanging down like red, swollen turkey wattles, unhesitatingly reached into the vials that stood in rows inside the open suitcase next to him and fed all of Killov's requests into the opened mouth, which waited like a bird to be fed. The officers walked in and looked down nervously, without making a sound.

Killov swallowed again and again, feeling the comforting objects squeeze down his constructed throat. He closed his eyes and waited. It didn't take long. As the pills and capsules dissolved, their chemicals entered his bloodstream and sent their magical effects throughout his system.

"Ah, yes, that is better," the KGB commander said, managing a grim smile for the first time in hours. He pulled away from his physician, who was still groveling over his lord and master, fully aware that Killov would remember this moment—would put the image of the doctor in his mind like a savior. Killov stood up, shakily at first since his spasming legs had to readjust to the streaming sensations that were shooting through his muscles and nerves.

"Yes, yes, much better," the top KGB'er said as he felt the wonderful, soothing chemicals fill his cells with painlessness, with artificial energy, with the power that fueled the madman and gave him life. Like a corpse returning from the dead, Killov walked around the room, half stumbling with his arms held out in front of him for balance as he tried to regain his equilibrium. The doctor and gathered brass looked on, smiling benevolently as if he were their child taking his first steps. Within minutes his body was functioning again, filled with the chemical pollution he thrived on, and his mind was as clear as the off-key crystal tones of a warped bell. He could feel the power entering him, recharging him, the waves of fuzzy warmth filling his heart and brain. The image of the ancient myth of Thor who had to but hold his immense hammer to the sky to be recharged by a fusillade of lightning bolts came into his mind. Yes, he *was* like that ancient fighter. For both of them — when filled with the godlike energy — were unstoppable.

"Now, first we shall take care of the mistakes that were made last night," the colonel said, walking to the wide leather chair of the previous Red Army commander of the fort, who was now in chains far below in the sub-basement. The chair was much too large for the ninety-pound body of the madman and he nearly slid out of it, but gripped the arm rests and settled himself.

"Who handled the transfer of my luggage? Which one of you?" His top six stood in a line on the far side of the mirror-polished wooden desk. Not a one could meet his burning, drug-fired eyes. "Which?" Killov screamed out, jumping up in his seat. "Tell me now — or you *all* die!" The line parted slightly as the officers backed off on each side from the man they knew to be the guilty party. Backed off, as if he had leprosy, as if just standing near him meant infection—death.

"Ah, so it was you, Kraskow. And I had thought you were going to work out so well when I appointed you one of my personal staff. When I took a chance on you just months ago. So, even I can be wrong." Killov looked at the man with false sympathy. "Ah well, it proves that I am only mortal, doesn't it?" he said with a dark smile. "And perhaps that is a good thing, is it not, Kraskow?"

The offending KGB'er had not the slightest idea of the proper response. He knew that Killov was toying with him—that though the man spoke softly, his life lay in the balance.

"Yes, Excellency—you are—mm-m-mortal," Kraskow stuttered, trying to phrase his words so that they might let him live. "But you are the pinnacle of mortals, the top of the mountain of humanity—so high that the gods themselves feel your power."

"How eloquent," Killov said sarcastically. "Really, I should have had you write my speeches not arrange for my luggage. Again, my mistake."

Kraskow relaxed ever so slightly as Killov's anger seemed to be dissipating. Perhaps the KGB leader, recognizing his intellectual powers, would in fact allow the officer to escape with only minor punishment.

"Yes, it is true," Killov said reflectively, "I am perhaps as close as man has ever come to the realm of the gods. It is a heady experience. Would you like to feel it for a moment? What it is like to touch the clouds, to sit in the seat of ultimate power?" He rose, walked to the side of the desk, and pointed toward the seat he had just been sitting in. "Please."

Kraskow looked like a man staring at his own grave. "No, really, Excellency, I don't think that I should—"

"Sit!" Killov shrieked, his face instantly going from chalk-white to beet-red. He rushed around the front of the desk, grabbed the officer by the arm, and led him back to the large leather armchair, pushing him down in it with the strength of the drugs coursing through his corpse-like arms.

"There—not so bad, is it?" the KGB commander asked the seated man. "Can you feel the power? Can you feel the energy surging down from the clouds—through the windows—filling your mind with perfect clarity, the vision of the stars?"

"I'm afraid, sir, that I really don't—" Kraskow began, speaking so quietly that he could barely be heard. The other officers watched nervously. They knew the depravities of which Killov was capable and although every one of them had murdered or been responsible for whole graveyards of death—there was something about the way Killov looked, the way his face truly did take on the fleshless characteristics of a skull, eyes dark as the empty reaches of space itself—that made them suck in their breaths, made their hearts beat wildly.

"Perhaps if you were more comfortable," Killov said with exaggerated politeness. "Perhaps you are afraid you will fall out of the chair and that is what is stopping you from feeling the power. You," the KGB colonel snapped out at the others, standing silently in the center of the room. "Tie him down with your belts to the chair—so that he will not fall."

Without hesitation the officers walked forward and against Kraskow's terrified protests, strapped him down to the chair with belts tied around his arms and legs. They pulled back and Killov again addressed the now-shaking officer, his eyes wide as saucers.

"Now—you know you did cause me pain, don't you?" Killov asked the man, addressing him almost tenderly as a parent would an errant child who had broken a plate.

"Yes sir, I know," Kraskow began, seeing his last chance to plead for his life. "It was my only mistake, Excellency. I have been a loyal and obedient officer. Why, just last month you gave me a commendation for—"

"Yes, yes, last month. But the past is dead along with all the bodies that lie buried in it. Last night— we are talking now about last night. Now I'm going to give you a great honor," Killov went on, walking around the desk with his hands clasped behind his back. As the drugs filtered into his bloodstream, his eyes grew narrower and narrower, his face flushed with the chemicals that raced through him. He searched for each word as if it were of critical importance that it be just the right one—as if he were reciting Shakespeare.

"Yes, a great honor. I suffered last night, Kraskow.

Suffered pains worse than death. And I found it in some ways quite educational. I am going to share *this* with you, my friend. Let you experience the glory of pain as I did. The enlightenment of suffering."

"Excellency, Excellency—my wife, my—" Kraskow sputtered.

"Shut up, pig. Your groveling merely shows that you have never been worthy of wearing the Blackshirt or the Deathhead pin that sits on your collar," Killov screamed out, reaching over and ripping the golden insignia of the KGB Officer Corps from Kraskow's lapel. The KGB leader stood back and looked at the offending officer as if contemplating a great work of art—trying to understand it, comprehend its every nuance. For Killov was, if nothing else, an artist of pain. Instruments of torture were his brushes and the human body was his canvas.

"Yes, I see it now," he whispered with delight. The full strength of the handful of chemicals he had swallowed was hitting him like a tidal wave—ripples of fire rushing through his screaming open veins, his vision slightly wobbly and hazed over with the soft pall of gray and gold he knew and loved so well. His lips had dried to white string beans, devoid of any color whatsoever; his cheeks were sunken in, valleys in which shadows gathered to die. His eyes were filled with the raging madness that the officers had seen before. It filled them to the very depth of their bowels with a sick and nauseated sensation. For in his madness, Killov had performed acts of torture that the stomachs of even the most hardened of his murderers could not take. Killov was the leader of them all in the infliction of such sensations. He led them into the darkest recesses of the human soul. Places where there was no sky, no God, no love or hope. Just sadism—sadism taken to an infinite degree.

"Yes, beautiful," Killov barked out, specks of yellow foam gathering around the corners of his mouth from the drug dehydration like the froth of a rabid dog. He clapped his hands. "Please gather around our esteemed colleague, Kraskow. Come, come," he snapped impatiently as they faltered. He made them stand just inches away from the seated figure, whose face was now washed from forehead to chin with a thin sheen of sweat and tears.

The KGB commander reached down suddenly into his boot and pulled out a long sharp single-sided blade with glistening steel flames of light racing along its edges.

"Now you see, it's really quite simple," Killov said, addressing his officer cadre as if they were pupils and he the headmaster. "To achieve maximum pain it is necessary to go right to the source. Some favor modern high-tech equipment and they do have their points—but I prefer to go right *to* the point." At the word "point," with a speed that startled those gathered, Killov whipped the blade in a blurred circle up and then down onto Kraskow's immobilized arm. The blade slammed clear through the wrist, the bone, and then into the wooden arm of the chair itself. The severed hand leaned over slowly, hanging by just a few sputtering veins, and then fell with a splat onto the floor.

Kraskow's face turned sheet-white as the hand fell. His eyes opened so wide that the officers could see the vein structure at the inner edges. It seemed as if he were taking the longest breath in history, just sucking and sucking at the air. Suddenly he released the air flow and let forth with a scream that made the hair crawl along the arms of the KGB brass.

"Yes, yes, see how he screams," Killov said proudly, pointing to his victim. Kraskow's forearm, just above the severed wrist, was spouting a torrent of blood that splashed over Killov's legs and boots and onto the officers' pants as well. Jaggedly sliced tendons and the stump of bone poked out at odd angles from he butchered appendage, as if not quite sure whether to stay or go.

"Now all we need," Killov said, licking his dry lips constantly with quick flickers of his narrow dark tongue, "is—" He looked around. "Ah, here." He smiled benignly at his students, barely able to see them now through the rushes of light and color that rode the river of drugs through his veins. "Electricity—such a wonderful thing." He reached over, unplugged a table lamp and slammed the knife down again on the cord where it entered the lamp-base. He took the exposed twin wires that had been feeding the lamp electricity and walked the several yards back to Kraskow who, even in the mindless screaming of his pain, knew he didn't like what was coming.

"Now, for the pièce de résistance," the KGB leader said, nearly falling over, but catching himself at the last second. "We apply the electricity to the source that will feel it the best." He held the shiny red copper wires right up to the dangling nerve bundles and ligaments that hung like limp bloody strings. "Drekoff, plug it in!" The wires sparked as they touched

45

the moist tissue and sent a blue arc of 220-volt electricity directly into Kraskow's nervous system. This time there was no hesitation in his reaction. The man's entire body jerked and convulsed within the straps of the chair as if he were coming apart from inside out. His face instantly went red as a boiling lobster as his tongue burst from his mouth, swelling larger by the second, the blood vessels in it popping and bubbling. The mutilated arm swung wildly around within its confines, sending a spray of blood over the entire audience like a hose.

"There, you see," Killov laughed with enthusiasm, "it works. The pain is—extreme, is it not?" The officers, coated with blood, tried to keep from vomiting, for they knew that to fail to show fortitude and appreciation in the face of Killov's hideous game meant that they might be the next game themselves. Twisted, grinding smiles somehow carved their way onto the officers' faces and Killov took it in, satisfied.

Kraskow's eyes began to boil and smoke came out of his ears in slow puffs. With Killov continuing to hold the wires to the stump, jamming them deep inside, the thing in the chair flopped, twisting in impossible angles. Suddenly the brain, heated to the boiling point with nowhere to go, exploded through the face. The nose, the eye sockets, the teeth and lips vanished beneath the ooze of pink and gray tissue. The crown of the skull parted, the super-heated brain erupted into the air, and over Killov and the officers.

Killov whipped the wires out of the twitching arm as it was obvious even to him in his drug-cooked madness that the thing that had been Kraskow was dead. The KGB leader looked around with the face of a rat that had just feasted on blood until its stomach is bloated and heavy, its face twitching.

"This is *the way of pain*. This is the law beyond laws. My law. You all understand, don't you?" He surveyed them one by one, checking for weaknesses, flaws, dangers. It was all part of Killov's chess game with those around him. Playing with their minds, exposing them to his bloody rituals and photographing their reactions in his memory for future reference.

"Yes, you understand. I can see it in your eyes." A radio watch beeped on Killov's wrist as a voice announced: "Excellency, the military council awaits your command at the War Room."

"Yes, perfect. Perfect timing," Killov responded, smiling indulgently at the officers. Murder always put him in a good mood. "I'm coming." Without brushing his clothes free of the red remains of Kraskow, Killov exited the room, followed by his officers.

Kraskow's body lay slumped in the chair. Below the waist the mess of a man looked normal enough, but above . . . the severed stump, the head virtually gone. Above the shoulders just the neck, the front of the jaw remained — and oddly, the lower portion of one lip set in a slight downturned expression of sadness. It looked like an abstract statue, as if it had been made out of clean, carved stone instead of human flesh and bone. A sculpture depicting the ultimate flaw of the human character: That there was nothing man wouldn't do to his fellow man.

Chapter Four

Rockson awoke, his head splitting like someone had just been chopping logs on it. Something was ringing loudly nearby. His watch — it was time for the meeting. Christ. He sat up and his skull felt like it was on fire. Every motion set his backbone into paroxysms of pain. Sometimes it was like that when he used the powers the Glowers had shown him. There was beauty in it, incredible beauty and understanding. But it took something out of him as well. He was not a Glower. Perhaps these headaches were a warning sign telling him to stop.

But by the time he was dressed and had splashed some water on his half-closed eyes, he felt slightly more human. He headed out the door and down the ramp system several levels to the Council Chamber. The meeting hall for the civilian and military leaders of Century City had been badly damaged in the neutron bomb attack of the subterranean city. But though the walls and much of the more ornate carvings that had been installed over the years had been carted away, the large oval-shaped auditorium was, if not beautiful, at least functional. Rock could see that the meeting had not yet really started as delegates marched around the chamber, cajoling and currying favor with their allies and enemies for whatever votes might be forthcoming. He started down the center aisle toward the podium and President Langford, who was sitting down, still not looking like something you'd stick in the window, when he saw Kim wave and start up toward him. But as she reached up to kiss him, Rockson saw another figure rushing up the aisle with a none-too-pleased expression on her perfect face. Rona Wallender.

"Pardon me, dear," she said icily to Kim, who looked up with a startled expression. "Might I give a hug from the Century City Welcome-The-Boys-Home Committee?" Rock, ready to take on a razor-snouted polar bear or Red battalion at a moment's notice, hadn't the slightest idea how to handle the situation — and just let his eyes roll up and his arms hang at his sides. The two women he loved — together in the same place. Somehow he had always known it was going to happen, but like earthquakes or volcanos, you don't look for them — they find you.

Rona pulled away from Rockson, smacking her lips lustily, and spun around toward Kim, her long red hair swinging wildly like strands of fire behind her. The two of them eyed each other like cats suddenly having to share a household in which one has been queen.

"So pleased to meet you," Rona said, poisoned sweetness dripping from her full lips. "I've heard *such* sweet things about you. And you *are* sweet. Why, you're just the cutest little thing." She looked over at Rock with a half snort of disgust that the man she loved would pick such a tweaky little thing—even though he *was* two-timing her.

Rockson kept his eyes focused on infinity as if, like an ostrich burying its head in the sand, that was somehow going to save him.

"And you, Kim said loudly, pushing her chest out, putting her clenched fists on her hips, "for all your muscles and your Amazon proportions, look—almost like a real woman."

Rona stepped forward, cocking a fist, ready to deck the blond bug before her with a single blow. At 5'10" plus, the one thing the statuesque acrobat and fighter was sensitive about was her well-developed physique. Sometimes in her most depressed moments she had felt that perhaps Rockson wanted a more feminine kind of woman—a petite charmer with dainty sex-kitten little movements and fickle tosses of the head. And Rona would never be that, could never play the coquette.

"But dear, you don't look healthy at all," Rona retorted, looking down at her rival, withdrawing her fist as she realized it wouldn't help her cause with Rockson to smash in the teeth of his paramour. "You really should eat more—your ribs, everything—that is, what little there is to see—is poking out. Meat—eat more meat, my poor little thing."

"She really is a remarkable specimen," Kim said, turning her big blue eyes to Rockson, whose headache was threatening to jump back into his head, combat boots first. "With those thick arms and huge legs, perhaps she's the female Homo Mutatiens, like you. Although from what you told me about Dr. Shecter's theories of post-nuke evolution, she looks

51

more like a throwback than a new species. Something more related to a Neanderthal, perhaps."

At the word Neanderthal, Rona threw herself through the air at her rival, and only Rockson's outstretched hand at the last second snatched her back by the hair as Kim raised her fists for a go at it. Rona turned around toward Rock, bringing her knee up toward his solar plexus as the chairman's gavel cracked loudly several times. He coughed and looked down at Century City's most renowned fighter and the two women who were about to set in tooth and nail. And even they had to soften under the stern gaze of council president Randolph, appointed recently after the disaster. He had a strong presence and had resolved to run all meetings under the full sway of the City's laws and rules of decorum.

"There will be no fighting in this chamber as long as I am council president," he said, severely admonishing the three of them, who melted under the words as hundreds of eyes peered over in astonishment from around the room. The trio, their faces red as burnished apples, sat down in the front row, not one of them daring to look at any of the others.

"And now that the little pre-meeting entertainment has ended," Randolph went on, "we can begin." The council president looked over suddenly to the right side of the stage and nodded his head quickly. A scratchy sound came over the P.A. system.

"Please rise," Randolph said, as the words of the Star Spangled Banner began. "Please rise to welcome the President of the United States, Charles M. Langford."

"Oh, say can you see,

52

By the dawn's early light . . ."

Every man and woman rose as Langford got up from his chair and managed to slap a smile of sorts on his face. He walked toward the podium and, as if remembering the charisma of days of old, held his hands high over his head in a victory sign. The delegates cheered, tears coming to their eyes. They had all thought they were as cynical as they came—but the sight of the first president of the U.S. had had for a century cut through the veneer of sophistication. A man voted into office by a free election held among delegates from virtually every Free City in the country. He was old, half beaten—but he was their president.

"Thank you, thank you," Langford said, obviously moved by the ovation. Rockson, standing with the rest in the front row, noticed that the man's eyes seemed to light up with a sparkle they hadn't had for weeks. Maybe, just maybe . . . Langford waved his hands up and down for the crowd to sit, but the people wouldn't. The applause went on and on. And when the song on the record player ended, it was put on again. There were few moments like this—having a sense of pride and a feeling of truly being a part of an all-encompassing America instead of just a collection of quarreling, isolated hamlets, never really getting it all together. Langford was the living symbol that it was all possible—every one of their impossible dreams of freedom.

After the second singing, the crowd at last quieted and sat down, but on the edge of their chairs.

"Thank you, thank you, I am deeply honored," Langford said in a low but firm voice. "Not just for myself, but for the office of the presidency, which I think is what you are really applauding, what you are really feeling." He exhaled, trying to regain his total concentration, as if coming out of a fog that had hovered over him.

"Now, I have no great words of encouragement to offer you. We're all grownups here. Have all been through the realities of present-day life. Things are hard—and getting harder. But I also sense a change. Something in the wind that says our day is coming. If we just work together, grow into something bigger than our separate parts—be like the America of old— indivisible, all fighting for and with all. We can win. In my heart I truly believe this. Our Soviet occupiers are at one another's throats. *We can win!*"

The delegates stood and cheered again as Langford seemed to tire suddenly and gripped the lectern with trembling hands. The crowd knew the words were clichés, generalities. But men lived by such and always had. For humans, above everything else, need hope or all is lost.

"Thank you, sir," Randolph said, stepping forward and taking the president by the elbow and leading him back to his chair. He returned to the front of the stage. "And I think I can say for all of us, not just here in the Council Chamber, Mr. President," he said, turning his head slightly toward the seated Langford, "but for every citizen of Century City, that we consider it a great personal honor to have you visit us here and want to let you know that you are welcome for as long as our facilities and personnel are of use to you."

The delegates let out a stomping roar of approval

for those words. The idea that they were, if only momentarily, the capital of Free America, that from within their granite walls plans and orders would be sent out to stir action in every part of the nation, was truly thrilling.

"But now, down to the business at hand. President Langford's words came at a very appropriate time, I must say," Randolph intoned grimly. "And to fill you in on just what the situation is around the country—I'll let Intelligence Chief Rath provide the update."

Rath came stage-center, greeted by a few half-hearted cheers as well as low grumbling boos. Rath, though a workaholic and highly efficient in his trade, was not a well-liked man. His personality was just a little too grating, and his need for 100% efficiency at all times from those who worked around him made him a hard and rigorous boss. But he got the job done. And in his business, that was all that mattered.

"We've received reports from our contacts all over the U.S.," Rath said, glancing down at a sheaf of notes in his hands. "And frankly, things look even worse than we had thought. Colonel Killov has apparently made great successes in his rebellion against the Russian military government here. President Zhabnov is either dead or has fled the country—but is nowhere to be seen. Rockson's attack on Killov and his forces in Washington has apparently forced them to flee the capital, which is now back in the hands of the Red Army. Killov is believed to be in Fort Minsk. As for the rest of the country, our estimates are that he and his men, turncoats and mercenaries, now control between 65% and 75% of all Red fortresses in America."

Gasps could be heard around the room. None of them had realized things were so bad. Zhabnov had been a buffoon, a joke. But Killov—that was a different story. If he truly became the unchallenged Red ruler of America—it was over.

"I would say gasps are in order," Rath said, letting the corner of his mouth turn up for a flash in a fraction of a sardonic grin. Then back to the pencil-straight expression that he wore eternally. "I would also say that the situation for Killov remains extremely unstable. He has taken, in some cases, fortresses containing up to 50,000 Red Army troops with his own attacking forces a tenth that size. But through surprise, the taking hostage of the entire officer corps of each fort, and the imprisonment or confinement to barracks of the lower ranks, he has thus far been able to keep a lid on the situation. As weeks go by, months—his hold will undoubtedly strengthen. And once he has a firm grip on the occupying forces—he will move against the Free Cities. And he will let nothing stand in his way."

"What is your recommendation for course of action?" council president Randolph asked from several feet away.

"Strike now, while there is still time," Rath spat out instantly, without thinking about it for a second. "This man cannot be allowed to get control of the Russian nuclear missile force over here. We must somehow launch an all-out attack on every one of these forts. As mad as it sounds—release the Red Army, free one enemy so that they can kick the other enemy, the KGB, right the hell into the dead zones."

Voices of protest rang out from the audience at the

concept of aiding the army that had burned and looted and raped and bombed out whole towns and villages in its constant effort to wipe out every trace of American resistance. The thought was repugnant to them.

As head of the City's combat forces, Rockson rose and stepped up on the dais.

"Request chair's permission to address the council," Rockson said, looking at Randolph.

The council president glanced around to see if there were any objections and, seeing none, said, "Take the floor."

Rock shuffled up to the center of the stage, squinting against the lights and the eyes of the delegates and civilians who packed the auditorium. He hated the limelight, and felt a deep blush threaten to slide up the side of his face. But those emotions were all bullshit when it was wartime.

"I'd just like to second Rath's feeling that we strike. We've been carrying out small attacks for years, getting nowhere, really. When I was your delegate to the Re-Constitutional Convention at which Charles Langford was elected president, one of the other things all the delegates agreed on was the need for a national military council—a coordinated effort in which we could use our forces as armies not guerillas. We fought the Neo-Nazis as an army, and won.* By uniting all the combat personnel of the larger Free Cities, we have nearly three-quarters of a million men ready to kick ass. The president's task force at

*See Doomsday Warrior #5.

57

Omicron City has developed contingency plans for quickly uniting all these forces. We have come together before, but never like this plan envisions. United we stand, divided we fall. Killov almost got us last time. Just look around you at the blackened walls, the broken seats you're sitting in. That's as close as you get and still talk about it."

"Course of action?" Randolph asked with a perturbed look.

"Call a national military council to meet here. Delegates—the top combat leaders of every city we can reach. We'll map out a massive surprise attack. All our armies, under one command, one central War Room. We'll attack, as Rath suggests. Help the regular Sovs throw out the KGB Blackshirts—and then retreat, causing as much damage to the Red fortresses as we can."

"And the Red Armies themselves—when they're freed?" Randolph asked. "We're talking about upwards of 2 or 3 million armed men."

"Well, I don't think we're ready for that battle right now," Rock said. "We'll do it on a fortress-by-fortress basis. As bad as Premier Vassily is, the man has at least stopped the use of nuclear weapons. Even the nuke-strike on Century City was Killov's undertaking. We can't let this nation take any more radiation. I've been out there—out in the wilds. America is wounded, damaged, but she's coming back. Slowly. But life and death still lie in the balance. No more atomic weapons can be used here. None—or the balance will tip and this country will slide into the dark ages."

There was a series of fervent shouts from the

audience as delegates who agreed and disagreed with the Doomsday Warrior let him know it with all their hearts. Rockson stepped from the stage. He'd said his piece. It was up to the men and women whom the people of Century City had elected to represent them to make the final decision.

After nearly two-and-a-half hours of intense debate—for Century City was, if nothing else, egalitarian to the hilt, preferring the screaming and occasional fist-fighting of pure democracy than the appointment of an ongoing leader, or a proxy system—they came to a decision. The motion carried—237 to 142—to convene a National Military Convention to prepare for "K" Day—when Killov and his KGB murderers would be sent back to their lairs. Free Cities around the country would be contacted by every possible means, including coded radio messages, carrier pigeons, and pony express. The meeting was set for exactly seven days from then, come hell or high water.

Rockson exited out the side, unable to deal with the two women he had left, who sat glaring at one another.

Chapter Five

Jed "Biscuit" Haverston flew around in the saddle of his big hybrid stallion like a buoy in a hurricane. It was amazing that the big tangle-bearded deerskin-clothed man could stay on at all, top-heavy as he was with rifles and ammunition, canteens and various pouches that hung over and around his large, round physique. And it was a lucky thing that the hybrid beneath him was as immense as he was — a good two feet taller and 300 pounds heavier than most 'brids — or it never could have carried the Pony Express rider for more than a few miles, let alone the hundred that they regularly trod.

Route 55, United States Pony Express System; and Jed was proud to be a part of it. In the ten years he had ridden for the organized and highly efficient delivery service, which was modeled after the Western postal carriers in America's days of old, Jed had logged in over 10,000 miles of service, carrying messages, gifts, gold coins — anything and everything that Americans in one Free City wanted to get to another. He had been bitten by snakes a hundred times, been attacked by wolves, coyotes, wild dogs, and Russians, not to mention the odd cannibal or two. Had lost six 'brids, had withstood rains, snows, tornados, earthquakes, and drought — all just to keep his part of the line going.

For "Biscuit" Haverston considered his job an honor, a part of building the new America, a blow against the Red occupiers every time he completed a successful delivery, every time he pulled up wild-eyed and exhausted, with his bags of precious cargo. And this — this of all carries — a call-to-arms for all Americans to rise, to take their guns and kick ass. He leaned forward astride the big steed, pressing his face and shoulder against the sleek muscular withers to cut the wind. The day he had been waiting for his whole life — for the Reds to be thrown the hell out — had finally come. And he was a vital part of that process.

"Come on, Eisenhower," Jed yelled to the hybrid. It had large hooves, as wide as dinner plates, and fur that covered them like those of some prehistoric mastadon or equivalent shaggy mammal of the Ice Ages. "We got a long way to go, fellow," Jed said, "and no time to do it in." After years of riding together, Jed swore that the animal could hear and understand him. They had an almost telepathic relationship, as many men and their animals do who've been through hell and back together. He could tell when the steed was tired, strong, thirsty, or just plain pissed off and ornery. And today, it was the last. For 'brids, like their human masters, had moods as varied

62

as the terrain they rode across—and it was vital that Jed understood them—and could use them to his advantage. Today, he knew that Eisenhower was mean. He had that wide-eyed look, that frisky bounce to his stride that Jed knew meant the creature was feeling its oats—probably thinking about some sweet mare that it wouldn't have minded spending a few passionate hours with. But Jed would use that energy. For like all living creatures, the animal's sexuality was the motor that drove it, and it could be channeled to other functions if one just knew how.

"Come on, boy, go, go," Jed said, leaning so close against the 'brid's side that he could feel its blood pumping, its iron-hard muscles pounding and coiling as it slammed its steel-shod hooves down on the parched prairie ground. He knew the 'brid's horniness gave it that extra strength, that electric energy that meant it could go and go fast. The landscape shot by them in a blur of sand and cacti as the Pony Express rider held on for dear life, keeping the reins loose and his legs tight as steel clamps around the sides of the speeding behemoth.

The sun tumbled from the sky in a bloody red mess and collapsed behind some far mountains as its silky white compatriot, the full moon, all decked out in her shining crater-pearls, rose into the rad-violet sky to take its place. Night was upon them in a flash as the sky grew as black as the bottom of the sea and a trillion speckles of silver paint splashed across night's ceiling. Tumbleweed blew across the flatlands like bubbles as the cool night wind whistled out the lonely song of the desert. Jed loved it out here. He wasn't meant to be around people, never was no good with women. But give him a fast 'brid, lots of ammo, and a wad of good chewing tobacco, and he came alive. Out here in the middle of nowhere with not a soul around, Red or American. Only him, the 'brid, the vast curve of the earth, and the moon lighting the way with a beacon of purest white, just for him.

They rode for hours, nothing changing, nothing seeming to grow closer or farther away. If he hadn't actually known that they were in fact tearing ass at a good 35mph, Jed would have sworn he and Eisenhower were mounted on one of them treadmills a farmer showed him once—used rats running inside, chasing food, to turn a small generator and light up his whole barn. But all that modern technology was too much for the Pony Express man. He fell into the trance of the long-distance rider, blending with the stars and the sands around him until he couldn't tell where he began and they left off. But he never tired or fell asleep. Not for a second. His eyes were wide open, his ears, all his senses reaching out to encompass every shadow, every howl in the dark. This was what he had been born for—and would die doing.

The 'brid suddenly slowed slightly and turned its head up and around toward him, moving its oversized lips furiously.

"Thirsty boy, huh?" Jed whispered in the animal's ear. "Yeah, you deserve a break." He sat up and scouted the terrain ahead for any signs of danger. There were no trees or hollows for predators to hide behind—just a few low moonlit hills off to the right—but he didn't see a living thing on them. He pulled the reins back slowly, patting the 'brid on the side.

"Whoa boy, whoa. You'll get your drink." The hybrid came to a complete stop and flung its head around from side to side, spittle flying out in a spiraling spray. Jed laughed at the animal's expression of thirst and jumped down from the saddle, grabbing one of five large gourds he had tied around the top of the 'brid's back where a whole array of supplies hung precariously from ropes and bags, somehow never quite falling off. Jed walked to the front of the towering creature and pulled the wide top off the gourd, holding the cool gallon of spring water up to Eisenhower's lips. It plunged in, slobbering half of it off in every direction as it attacked the gourd with a tongue the size of a first baseman's mitt. It got only half of the liquid down its gullet, but looked satisfied nonetheless. The big head arched around toward Jed and licked him along the face from neck to scalp, leaving the side drenched.

"No, dagnabbit—you can't get your oats now. When we get to Foster Station—then you can eat like a pig. But this is it, pal, and I ain't eating either. And you know *I* like to eat. So we're in this together. Understand?" The 'brid whipped its head around the other way in disgust and stood there, obviously pissed off.

Jed had put one foot up in the stirrup when he heard the noise. A low growling sound with a teeth-snapping edge to it that the Pony Express rider didn't like one bit. It was a carnivore—and it had him sighted.

"Easy boy, easy," Jed whispered, continuing to rise up toward the saddle, but slowly, very slowly. At the same time, he reached around with his right hand and

65

pulled one of the three rifles slung around his shoulder forward. By the time he was fully mounted on the 'brid, he had the hunting rifle under his arm, finger on the trigger. Jed kicked the 'brid in the sides with both boots and the animal started slowly forward, looking nervously over in the direction of the sound.

Suddenly it came again, but ten times louder—and attached to the hideous scream of hunger—the thing that had made it. Jed's eyes open wide in disbelief. He'd seen everything in his years of riding the Express—saber-toothed mountain lions as big as bears, snakes with wings, packs of rats that stretched off to the horizon. But he'd never seen a mutation like this. It had no face—or rather, it was all mouth. A row of jagged spiked teeth stretched from just below the ears, all the way across the bottom of the head. Hundreds of teeth in a set of jaws that looked like they could chomp a watermelon in half. Humanoid in shape, the thing's body was at least seven feet tall with legs the size of tree stumps, dark purple in color, and with arms as long and strong as a gorilla's with curving claws at the ends.

It came at Jed from about a hundred feet away, moving at amazing speed for a thing with its size and bulk. Jed knew he couldn't get the 'brid up to full speed in the semi-darkness with rocks around before the thing would catch them. They'd have to duke it out. He pulled the dusty Browning 8mm up to his shoulder and fired at the monstrosity, which howled as the slug caught it just beneath the shoulder—but it kept on coming.

"Oh shit," Jed muttered into the rising wind. He pulled the trigger again and again, sighting up the thing's head since its chest seemed impenetrable, covered with a thick leathery hide. The 'brid was rearing back now, unable to contain its fear any longer. But Jed hung on and kept shooting. Just ten feet from them, the thing stopped in its tracks, its head bleeding in torrents from the top of the skull. It let out a loud gurgling sound and toppled straight over toward them, its claws—which looked as if they could pluck a heart from a man—falling only inches short of the 'brid's hooves.

"Let's get the hell out of here," Jed shouted, turning the hybrid around and heading east again. But they'd gotten only fifty feet or so when more shapes emerged from the surrounding low rocks as if they were coming right up out of the earth. Jed saw one, then another—and within seconds a dozen of them, all as ugly as their deceased pal, all with the same thresher mouths, burning silver eyes, bright and wide as a cat's, staring at him—at his flesh—their teeth dripping with foul saliva.

"You ain't eating this Pony-Man," Jed screamed at the advancing line of carnivorous mutants. "You can forget all about that shit." He patted the 'brid softly. "Boy, you do this for me and I'm going to give you a whole bushel of applemelons—you hear me?" The 'brid had stopped in its tracks and was pacing nervously, slamming its front right hoof down on the hard-packed ground as if declaring its strength, its right to go ahead, to the approaching nightmares. "That's right—you and me—we're going to get outta this thing." He pulled both of the other rifles around front so he was cradling two under his left arm and one under his right, which also held the reins.

"Go, boy, run like your goddamned hairy ass never run before!" He kicked the animal hard in the sides and let out with a wild rebel yell, the kind his dad had taught him — a vocal vestige of pre-war days.

Eisenhower stood up on its hind legs and pushed its forelegs toward the meateaters like a boxer, ready to draw blood. Then it came down and shot forward, accelerating like a missile. The dozen or so surrounding mutations rushed at them from all sides, their claws slashing at the blur, their fangs snapping wildly at the air like meat grinders ready to pulverize anything. Holding himself atop the weaving back by squeezing his legs as tight as he could against the 'brid's side, Jed fired all three of his rifles at once. Two of the attackers fell to the ground moaning, as a third kept coming — but with the whole side of its face missing as if it had just dropped off. Claws dug in along the hybrid's flank and Jed felt a stabbing pain in his right thigh as a row of six-inch daggers sliced along his side like a carving knife into Thanksgiving turkey. But the 'brid just kept going as if nothing was there and suddenly they were past them.

"Good, good boy," Jed laughed out loud, rubbing the hybrid's ear furiously. He slung all three weapons back around his shoulder with one toss and grabbed hold of the reins, leaning forward again around the animal's shoulder to protect himself from the now-freezing midnight winds. With much of the protection of the atmosphere gone now, burnt away by radioactive acids, the nights were much colder in America. It was as if the dark seas of space itself fell onto the earth at night, chilling it to the very granite marrow of its bones. But protected by the golden mane and the wide neck of the hybrid which shielded him from the wind, and wrapped up in five layers of longjohns, shirts, feather vest, and beaver coat, he figured he was ready for everything, including the next Ice Age.

They rode through the night, Eisenhower flying along as the animal found its perfect pace. The encounter with the maneaters had, if anything, pumped some adrenaline into its system and it galloped in a perfect synchronization of legs and breath. Puffs of frosty smoke blew from its mouth and nose like the mechanized releases of a factory. Even through his clothes Jed could feel the immense amount of heat the beast was generating through its efforts. The stars moved slowly like weary travelers searching for but never finding a home to rest in along the lonely reaches of the galactic highway. The moon sank to its bed, tired, ready to curl into a fetal ball in the black blankets of Mother Earth. And then the sun inched into the sky, bright and ruddy, promising the world the warmth of a new day.

But Jed felt a sensation other than heat—a pain in his leg—and in his guts. He hadn't stopped to check the wound he'd suffered from the claws of the "big mouth," and the 'brid hadn't complained. But now—now the leg felt—strange. Within seconds of the initial burning sensation of pain, Jed's eyes grew unfocused, his head soft and confused. What was happening? Poison—somehow the thing had released a poison into him. He tried to stop the 'brid, reaching forward for the reins, but felt his limbs become paralyzed, his muscles tight as steel cables. The last thing he remembered was his face falling into the soft golden mane of Eisenhower.

The hybrid knew something was wrong. Master was still, hadn't moved for hours. The animal felt the edges of a numbness in its body—the poison injected from the hollow claws of the unhumans—but its powerful system, able to take just about anything that nature had to offer, kept on ticking. It slowed to a medium trot, keeping its body as straight as possible so that Master wouldn't fall. It couldn't help him, give him water, minister to him in any way; dimly it knew that. It had only an instinct—to get to the next Pony Express station some fifty miles ahead. This was the most treacherous part of their journey— earthquake chasms as easy to fall into as a pool of quicksand. But it had traveled the route for as long as it could remember, and the highly intelligent animal knew the ground by heart. It moved on, carrying the unconscious rider as carefully as a load of eggs.

There—the stream. It always felt happy at the stream, for there was clear pure water and it meant that the desert part of their trip was over. It stopped by the banks of the rambling trout-filled cascade and carefully lowered its head, inch by inch, making sure that the Master didn't tumble headfirst into the wetness. It drank, long and hard, letting the water chill its long throat, pour down into its stomach until it felt almost bloated. At last it stopped and raised its head high as if acknowledging the noonday sun. It was hungry, starving. But there would be food later. It had to move on.

Two hours later, it recognized the start of the winding rocky trail that led over the edges of an ancient A-bomb crater—a contender for title of heavyweight atomic crater of the world at twenty megatons. It had a mouth as big as a primeval volcano, nearly two miles wide with steeply sloping sides that rose up half a mile into the air. The 'brid carefully made its way around the side of the war mountain, rising higher and higher along the man-made trail. At first the going was easy, but as it rose into the sky the narrow path grew steeper and rockier until every step was tricky. The 'brid remembered that once it had almost fallen down the side of this crater. It had come too near the edge of the yard-wide trail and its hind leg had gone off the side, releasing a mini-avalanche of rocks and debris down the slope below it. But somehow, with Master pulling and the animal frantically clawing with its other three legs, it had gotten itself back up. The memory glowed as if branded into its brain.

At last it reached the summit and turned around for a moment on the rimwall, surveying the land they had traveled across. Jed always did it — and now the hybrid did it as well, from habit. Then it started across the wide lip of the crater, where all sorts of small flowers grew and birds had chosen to build their nests. The feathered creatures put up a chirping chorus of indignation and alarm as the giant passed through their twig-and-straw condo's. It walked the craters edge, reached the other side just as the sun hit the horizon and started down.

Haverston stirred. *What* — he remembered. Poison! The 'brid was still moving. Blearily he could see they had come far. "Good boy," he rasped. With his mind fighting the desire to fall back into unconsciousness, he managed to strap himself on the saddle. Then —

darkness.

The floodlight of the full moon, which sliced down through a thin layer of green strontium clouds high in the stratosphere, lit the side of the crater with a garish brilliance, so the hybrid could see every square inch ahead of him. Placing one wide foot after another, it made its way down the slope, moving between boulders and cracks and sheets of gravel ready to slide away at the slightest motivation. But the 'brid had always felt more comfortable on this side of the crater anyway, almost playing at some points, as it would slide for yards at a time down a loose layer of sand. At last it reached bottom and immediately headed straight for the thick woods which began on the base of the eastern slope of the nuke hole and stretched on for a good twenty miles. It hit the woods in a flash and started down the wide logger trail that had been carved out a century ago. The shadows created by the branches lit from above by the wild eye of the moon made it nervous. It remembered again how it feared the woods in the darkness. And with Master asleep, there would be no loud noises, no flashes of white — and then blood. There would be no protection but its own stone-hard hooves and chomping-flat teeth — and its speed.

If an animal can feel fear, knowing something *may* attack it, then Eisenhower felt fear. And if an animal can feel courage — overcoming its fear to advance onward — then the 'brid exhibited the same. For it marched through the low overhanging branches filled with a million leaves, twisting its long neck from side to side, trying to keep every square inch of the semi-darkness in view. From time to time it could see fiery eyes glowing back at it from the shadows. But it would just speed up and keep on going, never slackening for a moment, never letting down its guard.

Suddenly it saw five shadows, motionless, waiting. The 'brid knew by the low, white furred bodies that they were wolves. It had been attacked by them before—but Master had destroyed them. Now they waited, knowing there was no way off the trail, that the woods were too thick and densely woven for a creature as large as this mutant descendant of the horse family. Eisenhower looked back at the trail behind him and saw three more shapes lope down from the woods and start up the wide dusty animal-made pathway.

In its primitive heart the hybrid felt the urge to panic, to thrash its forelegs wildly, to buck and stomp. But in its mind, a mind honed and taught by the Master, it knew better. To stay was to die. To fight was to die. There was only one way. Gathering its strength, the 'brid snorted a whale-like puff of smoke through its steaming nostrils, clapped its front right hoof against the ground three times, and then started forward. One of the most notable attributes of many breeds of the 21st-century hybrid horse is its ability to accelerate. With upper thigh muscles as wide as a man's chest, the animals can put out a prodigious amount of accelerative energy in a very short period of time. With just fifty yards to go until it reached the waiting jaws of the wolf pack—now sidling carefully forward, their heads down, their shoulders hunched, checking out the prey and the best way to kill it—the great mass of pure muscle took off like a racehorse from the wire. It pushed down harder, stronger with every ringing clap of its hooves on the hard ground. At fifty feet it had hit 25mph; at a hundred feet, 35. It came at the wolves with a steely look in its eyes — ready to die if it had to, but knowing it would take a field of carcasses with it.

The wolves suddenly grew fearful, high-pitched squeals of confusion emanating from their vicious jaws. They barked at one another, trying to figure the thing out — how to cut it off. But the 'brid wasn't about to give them time. It came on, its mouth wide, its feet pounding like exploding shells going off every time its weight came down on them. The wolves formed a wall, realizing that they had to stop it fast or they'd go hungry tonight. But the 'brid just came on at the pack, whose long incisors glistened in the spears of moonlight streaking down through the sky. The steed came right up to them and with a final thrust, using all of its power, leaped into the air with its hind legs. Like a jumper clearing the tallest hedge at Heathrow, the mutant horse went clear over the wolves' backs, coming down yards past them on the other side. The predators whipped around in confusion, trying to gather themselves, and took off with a halfhearted charge after the galloping animal. But it was already gone, leaving only a cloud of slowly settling dust.

Eisenhower didn't slacken the pace for a good three miles, looking back every few hundred yards to see if there was anything following. But there wasn't. Just eyes which continued to track him from the endless tangles of brush and tree. He was going on pure adrenaline now, but knew that he had to pace himself. He couldn't make it if he maintained this momentum.

The steed slowed to about half its speed and settled into that as if shifting to a lower gear. It could feel weariness creeping over it like a spider web of dull warmth through its body, its dirt-coated legs. But the Master was still not moving. Now *it* was the Master.

By the time the sun once again pulled itself up on thin yellow arms over the ledge of dawn, the hybrid had come out of the thick forest and back onto open land, lush with flowers and ponds and small animals already creeping out into the mist-covered morning to search for food. Close—it was close to the station. It could feel it ahead and the desire for food, for rest, pulled it inexorably forward like iron filings toward a magnet. It crossed several miles of low fields and then skirted a wide oval lake where large dark shapes swam just below the surface—waiting.

At last the Express station was in sight. Even from a mile off the 'brid could see the people moving about, the smoke rising from several of the small log shacks that sat in a defensive circle. The animal tore down a cleared road, avoiding the deep ruts of wagon wheels on each side, and came barreling in toward the depot like a cannonball looking for a place to land.

"Whoa, easy, big fella," a voice yelled out as hands flew up to grab the reins. The 'brid let them take control. They were not enemies, the were the Masters, the feeders.

"Lookee here," the man shouted out as the rider, still unconscious, fell into his arms. "It's Jeb Haverston—and he's hurt bad, real bad. Check his message-bag!"

Even as they tended to the unconscious—but not

mortally wounded—man, four other riders threw saddles on their own mounts and grabbed gourds of water. The Express had to go on. Within minutes the four were off to the north, east, south, and west to spread the word that K-Day had arrived.

Chapter Six

They came from out of nowhere. From wretched thatched-roof hovel-towns, from mini-cities as advanced and technologically proficient as Century City itself. They came by hybrid and mule, by ancient rusted cars and bicycles, a few even in stolen Soviet choppers. They carried high-caliber machine guns or just bows and arrows—but they came, ready to give whatever they and their Free Cities had to offer, to answer the call of the president of the Re-United States.

Ted Rockson, standing off to one side of the main square of the subterranean city, couldn't help but chuckle as he watched the groups of America's finest move among the crowd like little schools of differently colored fish. Each town and city had its own version of the proper combat gear, and the men strutted among one another like peacocks, showing off their stuff. The Texas fighters with their wide ten-gallon hats and six-guns strapped to each leg hooted and hollered across the floor, spinning lariats around one another, showing their expertise in the American sport of lassoing. The Kansas City Brigade wore suits and narrow leather ties—useful for garroting—and looked like businessmen of the last century, ready for a board meeting. Only their Uzis betrayed the fact that they were fighters, not 20th-century account executives. There were men in full U.S. Marine regalia, in Navy gear, in moth-eaten olive-drab Army uniforms. An all-Black unit from the outskirts of the ancient city of Detroit was dressed in black jumpsuits and bristled with knives, pistols, and smgs that were slung around their necks. They looked as tough as nails, but mingled with the other U.S. fighters smiling, their hands extended in friendship.

The various groups of disparately attired Freedom-fighters didn't quite know what to make of one another. But they knew that they had all been out there—fighting, bleeding, seeing their pals die, and waiting for their own incoming hell. And that made them brothers, instantly and forever. Brothers of blood and shrapnel. They showed their weapons to one another, marveling at some feature or other of a pistol or a rifle or a hidden spring blade. War stories were the main order of the day. How many this one had killed. How many Russians, tanks, convoys, and fortresses had been attacked. All the statistics that would fascinate a fighting man and bore everyone else to death. By the time the meeting was called to order, they were laughing and shadow-sparring with one another like boyhood buddies. This might be the only time they would meet. And most would die—of that they were all sure. So their exchanges of friendship and joking had special meaning for every one of them. A memory to clutch hold of when they were lying somewhere in a ditch with their guts smoking out of a hole in their stomachs.

"May I introduce the President of the Re-United States," council president Randolph said loudly, cutting through the chatter like a sword. All mouths closed and eyes turned toward the haggard-looking man who walked slowly to a hastily erected stage in the center of the wide Lincoln square. Seats had been brought from every part of the city and arranged in long curving lines around the central platform. They had expected several hundred — but nearly a thousand men had shown up, in some cases the entire top echelon of some of the Hidden Cities — all wanting to make the historic trip. Now they filled the entire square, stretching off for twenty rows. And the citizens of Century City, fascinated by the proceedings as well, stood far back against the concrete walls or sat atop the one-and two-story factories that surrounded the central thoroughfare. They broke into wild applause that once again brought a smile to President Langford's face. Rockson could see that the love and respect of his people really did seem to put some electricity back into the man's face. Kim sat up on the dais behind her father, so Rock at least didn't have to worry about being caught between two beautiful women attempting to throw haymakers at one another. Rona sat by his side, her arms through his, with a snide smile on her perfect face. She kept glancing up at the president's daughter, making sure she could clearly see who was with the man they both desired. For possession in love is nine-tenths of the law.

President Langford gave a rousing speech about heroism in the face of impossible odds and how proud he was of each and every one of them. The words were poetic and stirring, but the voice cracked from time to time. Yet it hardly mattered to those who listened. For he was *their* president — a living symbol that all was possible, that freedom was not just another pipe dream. So they gazed up at the old man as if he was the most beautiful thing they'd ever seen. All their days of fighting, of suffering, suddenly seemed worth every second of pain.

When Langford was finished, he walked slowly back to his chair and sat down with a thin smile beside his daughter, who was the only one who realized how weak he was, who saw how fast the man was failing. The delegates from the Free Cities were ecstatic, stamping their feet like teenagers at a rock concert.

"And now," council president Randolph said, stepping up to the podium, "I will give the floor to the man who probably has his finger on more of what is actually going on right now around the country than anyone — our intelligence chief, Frank Rath." The delegates yawned and scratched their chests and stomachs, eyes half closing as if they were ready to take an afternoon nap. They were fighters, most of them — with short attention spans and an eye for food and women. They had traveled with no notice, for days, to get here. But all of them knew that they had to rise to the pinnacle of their mental abilities. What they heard here, and their interpretation of the results, would have a drastic effect on the future of America as a nation of free men — not slaves. Thus, they were on their best behavior, pinching themselves to stay awake, sitting tall on the narrow wooden seats, and listening with every ounce of attention.

"Thank you, thank you," the tall gaunt Rath said, "please curtail your applause." He placed a folder filled with the latest intel reports of the evolving situation on the lectern. "Let's dispense with all the usual 'how happy I am to see you here's' and all that. We're here for one reason and one reason only — to forge a military response against the KGB forces that have taken over 65% of all regular Red Army fortresses in America." He reached down and lifted a gridded piece of paper showing the most up-to-date placement of Killov's troops, fortresses in the hands of the Red Army, and those bases still in dispute.

"Killov has finally made his move," Rath went on, looking down with a grim expression at the audience. "And thus far, his gamble has paid off. Zhabnov has fled back to Moscow and not only has Killov taken control of many fortresses, but he was able to take D.C. with all its central Red Army control centers and top military staff. Ted Rockson, who I might add is seated right now in the front row, was able to not only free the president but kick Killov's butt right the hell out of there. So as a byproduct of the rescue — the regular Red Army in D.C. has been able to take things over again."

The audience applauded lustily, but looked confused. The Red Army had always been their enemy. And now . . . "I know it's a weird situation," Rath went on. "We've been shooting their goddamned asses for a hundred years and now we have to try to free them from the KGB — who, as you all know from personal experience — are a thousand times more ruthless than even the most bloodthirsty Red Army commanders. And it's worse than just a KGB military takeover. Our agents report that one of Killov's priorities is gaining access to the landbased nuclear missiles that are scattered around the country. Thus far, due to elaborate security measures instituted by Premier Vassily, Killov has been unable to get to them—find their locations, break into them, get the code books that are needed for launch . . . But it's only a matter of time. And not much time at that."

"Why don't we just take all of them goddamned KGB butchers and the Red armies—all at once?" a voice shouted from the crowd. Ordinarily Rath would have scowled "Out of order!" Like Randolph, he was a decorum freak—but even he recognized that the times called for speed, quick debate, and total comprehension of the situation.

"We can—but I'm sure we'd lose," Rath said slowly and deliberately. "As I say, it's a peculiar situation. Killov's forces are outnumbered by up to fifty to one in some cases. But you see, the very thing that The Skull is master of is intimidation. He rules by fear and confusion. Most of the regular Red troops probably don't even really understand what's going on. The KGB—by decree going back to before the 1989 nuke war, has the freedom to go into any Russian military fortress in the world to search for traitors, saboteurs, blasphemers of the Communist orthodoxy. In the last few years, Killov apparently used this power more and more frequently, giving the Reds a chance to get used to it. To hate it, yes, but to accept it as an ongoing occurrence. This time, the KGB madman moved in a blitzkrieg, sending in commando teams by paradrop, at all the larger fortresses. Before they

could even respond, the officers, the munitions—
everything that controls the power within a fortress—
were in KGB hands. The ordinary Red soldiers are
being 're-educated,' and commanded now by a combi-
nation of KGB officer staff and those Red Army
commanders who have come over to what they see as
the winning side."

"Get 'em all, kill 'em all," another voice shouted
from far in the back.

Rath shook his head. "We might take on the actual
KGB units in a fort," Rath said, "but realistically,
with the number of men we'll be able to raise and
have combat-ready in the field within two weeks, we
wouldn't stand a chance against those caged-up army
units. Just their sheer number would overwhelm us
like carpenter ants over a grasshopper. We have no
choice, gentlemen—whether our stomachs like it or
not—but to get those fortresses back out of the hands
of the KGB. Otherwise it won't matter what you
think—not when Killov gets control of enough nukes
to start blasting all over the damned place. This
country will be deader than a doornail within months
if that happens. You all know that. You all know
what would happen to the little bit of life that has
been able to force its way back if a hundred A-bombs
were scattered around spitting out yet more poison."
He paused and looked around. "Let's use whatever
strength we have to prevent Killov from winning the
Red Civil War. Let them, *help them* destroy themselves. Then we move in when they're weak."

"I don't like it," a deep voice growled out from one
of the rear chairs.

"I don't like it neither," another, then another cried

out in a chorus of negation. Within seconds the place was roaring with yells, protests, and anger. The fighters could hardly believe what they were being asked to do.

"Please, please!" Rath yelled out, his hands raised high as the place threatened to erupt into bedlam. Already some of the less sophisticated Freefighters were standing on their chairs, their fists clenched, ready to take on any man in the joint.

Suddenly a figure rose from the seats and jumped on the stage. He walked past Rath and to the front of the platform. Without a word, he stared down at them, a palpable fire of fury burning in his mismatched violet and aquamarine eyes. Slowly, under the gaze of Ted Rockson, the crowd stopped moving and came to a hush.

"That's better, much better," Rockson said, as if addressing a class of twelve-year-olds. "Now please be seated. Not only is the president of your nation watching this debacle, but you are also guests of Century City and therefore of mine. And we don't allow anything but sport-fighting here. And we also consider it quite rude for people to yell when others are talking. You will all get your chance to be heard, I promise you. But you'll do it *our* way. Okay? If anyone wants to yell or fight, come up here on stage, right now, and we'll settle it—you and me, personal style." He looked around the audience of tough, hardened fighters, but not a one would take up the challenge. For they had all heard of the Rockson, the Ultimate American—even those in straw-strewn pigsties, out in the middle of nowhere. And not one had the desire, or the inclination, to tackle the job. He had made his point.

"Good," Rockson said softly, his every word cutting like a bullet through the suddenly silent air. "Now if you thought that Rath's idea was bizarre and unappetizing for your gourmet palates, try *this* on for size: I suggest that not only do we carry out the plan for liberation of the Red Army from KGB forces, but that we contact Premier Vassily in Moscow—and have him ally with us to fight Killov the common threat." There were gasps of shock from the fighters—but not one yelled out. "Because to be perfectly honest with you all, I don't think we can carry this thing out without additional, heavy-duty help. And from the lack of discipline demonstrated by many of you, I feel more convinced that my preconceptions were right."

Even Rath seemed shocked by this idea and looked at Rockson in confusion. "But—how, Rock? How could we possibly pull something like that off—and even if we could, how do we have any guarantee that the Reds wouldn't immediately turn on us as soon as the KGB had been vanquished? It's like fighting a wolf by swinging rattlesnakes in both hands."

"I've met Vassily," Rock said, addressing both Rath and the audience. "He's a tyrant—but he's neither a madman nor a fool.* Whatever he *does* want—he *doesn't* want the world destroyed. I know that. I think we can strike a deal."

"So what are you suggesting?" Rath asked, his face slowly draining of blood as he realized that Rockson was 100% serious.

*See Doomsday Warrior #4.

"I propose that I contact Premier Vassily and set up a situation for him to have Russian forces fight *alongside* American forces. And in exchange for that aid—we get the withdrawal of all nuclear weapons in America." Rockson stepped back, looked at Rath with a poker face, and let the intel chief take over.

"I open the floor to debate," Rath declared, setting an avalanche of questions and oppositions in motion. The often raucous meeting lasted for hours with every possible point of view being expressed. But as the debate yelled its way on, slowly it dawned on even the dimmest-witted of the fighters that in reality, they didn't have a hell of a lot of options.

As the city's largest clock, mounted halfway up the wall of the northern side of the square, hit 6:00 A.M., council president Randolph decided it was time for a vote.

"We've been over and over all the major proposals for hours now," he said, wearily addressing the throng. "I think it's time to decide—or it will be decided for us. Basically, as I see it, it comes down to three plans. Number One: we don't do a thing—let them fight it out. Continue to monitor the situation.

Number Two: we attack the KGB, not the Red Army. But *no* attempt to ally ourselves with Vassily.

And Number Three—Rock's plan: we arrange a temporary alliance with Premier Vassily, and fight alongside his soldiers to defeat Killov, our common enemy."

"Who votes for plan one?"

A smattering of hands went up.

"Plan two?"

This time a good quarter of the audience threw up hands and cheered mightily.

"And plan three?"

The vast majority of Freefighters raised their arms and let out a roar of victory. They voted for it because it was Rockson's plan and the man had worked miracles countless times—and because they were bone tired and could think of nothing finer than heading off to the rows of air-mattresses the people of the city had thrown together in the large gymnasium, and laying their heads down and sleeping.

Rath, who voted for Plan Two, was aghast. He thought when it comes to choosing between the higher intellectual faculties of man and indulging his baser animal instincts—the growl is mightier than the thought.

He would work to undo Rockson's mad scheme.

Chapter Seven

"Read it to me again, Rahallah," the shriveled Premier of All-the-Soviets said as he sat, eyes closed, in his wheelchair on the veranda of his office within the Kremlin, looking out over the Red Square.

"But Excellency, I've read it five times now," his black servant, dressed in full white tuxedo and gloves, answered, leaning forward and adjusting the blankets around Vassily's shoulders and lap. The premier looked ill again—very ill. But then Rahallah could hardly remember the last time the man had been vigorous, red-cheeked. He hovered between being able to work and meet with officials for three or four hours when he was at his best, and slipping into a semi-coma where he just slept, not responsive to stimuli, at his worst. Somehow the affairs of a world empire dragged on, run at the very top by a frail old man, his face dotted with age spots, his hands trembling, barely able to sign the documents that kept it all going.

"Yes, read it once more—that will be the last time," Vassily said, hardly moving his lips as he spoke.

"Very well then, sir," said Ruwanda Rahallah,

descended from African princes. He opened the book in his hands, the proscribed Holy Bible, to the page he had been reading and rereading to Vassily.

"And I beheld when he had opened the sixth seal, and lo, there was a great earthquake; and the sun became black and the moon became as blood;

"And the stars of heaven fell unto the earth, even as a fig tree casteth her untimely figs when she is shaken of a mighty wind.

"And the heaven departed as a scroll when it is rolled together; and every mountain and island were moved out of their places.

"And the kings of the earth, and the great men, and the rich men, and the chief captains, and the mighty men, and every freeman hid themselves in the dens and in the rocks of the mountains.

"And said to the mountains and rocks, Fall on us and hide us from the face of him that sitteth on the throne.

"For the great day of his wrath is come; and who shall be able to stand?"

Rahallah finished and closed the brittle rare book gently, thinking that Vassily was dozing since his eyes were shut as tightly as ancient crypts. He stood up, slid the glass door open, closed it, and walked to the edge of the stone-walled Kremlin terrace and looked down over the bundled commissars heading home in the slowly falling Moscow snow, making them look blurred, the colors of their clothing bleeding together as if in a 19th-century Impressionist painting.

"Do you know who the 'He' is in those passages, Rahallah?" Vassily asked, startling his African servant who had been deep in somber thought. The aged man had wheeled himself over to the glass door and opened it.

"Why, I would think it's—it's God, Excellency," Rahallah, turning replied. Theoretically no one could even read the Bible any longer—it was an outlawed "lie," as were countless thousands of other books. But Vassily was himself above all the laws for the common man. He was the leader of the world and had to have knowledge from every source to make the proper decisions. It wasn't that he believed in God, although as he grew older and sicker and closer to death, he was beginning to wonder—but more that he *did* believe in the ability of ancient humanity to divine the future. For many of their prophecies, those of Nostradamus and of the *tertons* of Tibet, had come to pass.

"It's not God, my faithful servant," the premier said with a long sigh. "It's Killov. I know it is. And those words you read to me are predicting the destruction of the earth. My fool nephew President Zhabnov was unable to keep control of the U.S. capital, even outnumbering the Dark One a hundred to one." Vassily coughed violently as he grew angry at the fat president of the United Socialist States of America. His blood pressure began rising dangerously. He coughed spasmodically.

"Grandfather," Rahallah gasped, rushing to him. "You mustn't strain yourself, mustn't grow angry or—"

"Why does it not stop, Rahallah?" the premier cried out in anguish. "Why is there no rest—for me—but always war, blood, and more blood? I am growing tired of it all, my only friend. I don't know how long I can keep things going, keep this decrepit old body from crumbling into dust."

"Grandfather," Rahallah said sternly, shaking a long white-gloved finger at the old man, "don't even talk like that. Half of life is wanting to live, *desiring* to stay alive, to see the next day, another sun, another flower. You must want to live — or surely you will die. And both of us know," the tall, strikingly noble-featured black man went on, "what your death will mean — for me, for Mother Russia — for the world."

"I *do* know," the premier said angrily. "You think I don't? That is why I continue to live when my flesh calls me to the grave. I feel the weight of the responsibility like a ton of bricks on my back. And it only adds to the weight, Rahallah. Only makes this frail flesh carry a heavier load than it can stand, until my back feels as if it were literally cracking and my legs as if they were made of gruel and water, not muscle and bone. I would have welcomed death long ago — were it not for the bastard Skull." Vassily threw his right hand over his face as if he were about to cry.

"Wheel me to the wall," he barked out suddenly, trying to distract his own emotions from consciousness. Rahallah complied instantly, pushing the elaborate stainless-steel wheelchair with reading lights, radio, drugs, hypodermic needles, and other paraphernalia onto the infra-red-heated terrace, over to the low wall with its troll-like gargoyles surrounding, as if guarding it from attack. Vassily stared out over the spires of Moscow, the thousand little funnels of smoke sweeping up out of the chimneys as women cooked the evening meal for their husbands and children. Between the momentarily breaking clouds, the setting sun sent golden arrows, cascading off the ancient Tsarist buildings that seemed to withstand the hands of time, the hands of different economic systems, different dictators. Even the prevalent radiation didn't seem to bother them.

At first, when he had grabbed the reins of power many decades before, the job had seemed thrilling, the fulfillment of his destiny. He had taken to running the world as a fish takes to water. His iron will, coupled with his inherent charm and sense of style and diplomacy, made him perhaps the most effective and benign ruler of all the Soviets since the nuke-war. Not that his subjects, spread around the world in their muddy little towns and villages, realized it. But he knew that in relation to what had been — and what could be — he was probably the best. And yet — now it all seemed in vain. All his efforts to loosen things up — if just a little. To stop nuclear weapons from ever being used again. It had all been just a holding action while Killov bided his time.

"Damn," Vassily swore, slamming one blue-veined, child-sized fist into the other. "I should have killed him when I had the chance. Many years ago, Rahallah," Vassily said, his eyes continuing to stare straight out at the spiraling rooftops, the statues rising into the darkening sky, bursting with blues and deep purples as blackness slowly oozed down from above like a bottle of fallen ink. "Many years ago, when the madman was trying to seize the reins of the power in the KGB when the previous commander died — or more probably, was assassinated — I sided with Killov in the battle, thinking at the time that he was the easiest to control, just because he was the youngest.

But I was wrong. By Lenin, was I wrong!" He let his head drop forward again, burying it in both trembling hands.

"Then stop him now—in his tracks. Send in troops from the Motherland to attack—before Killov gains complete control of his situation," Rahallah pleaded desperately.

"I wish I could," Vassily moaned, burying his head even deeper in his palms like a mole searching for a tunnel. "But the military situation is very bad throughout the Asias, North China, Japan, the . . . But why go on—there is no way I can spare Red Army troops. The empire is in turmoil. Every day there are more rebellions, more attacks on convoys, bases. It seems as if every woman, child, every little infant, hardly able to walk, has a gun in his hand. They hate us so. *Why* do they hate us so? Hate *me* so, Faithful One?" the premier implored the black servant, looking up suddenly at him, peering directly into his face as if searching for a savior.

"They hate you because they have no land of their own, no power of their own, no . . ."

"But I give them food, shelter. More food than all my predecessors put together. I have tried to stop unnecessary brutality, torture."

"It is not enough, Great One. Men need more than just a roof and a loaf of bread. They need—freedom."

"I cannot, I cannot," Vassily groaned as if in great pain. "You don't understand, no one understands. I have been put in charge of a great factory and must keep it moving. Keep its gears meshing together, keep its products, its food, churning out, keep the barbarians at bay so that they don't batter down the walls. If I were to give up the controls of the factory — it would stop, the machines would crumble, there would be only anarchy everywhere. The entire planet hurt mortally as it is by the radioactive result of the great war, would revert to the days of caveman, snarling and grabbing for the few bits of raw meat. Man was not meant to be free. He has never been able to use freedom properly. No, Rahallah, man was meant to be ruled, he longs to be ruled, by one empire, to be told what to do. And this is why I cannot hand back, scatter the reins of power. It would be like handing the reins to a wild horse — it would just wander freely, eating grass, sleeping in the snow until it froze to death. Man *needs* to be enslaved, faithful servant — it is but a question of who the master shall be."

"Then be prepared, Excellency," Rahallah went on, knowing that he might anger the premier, but knowing as well that his was the only voice of reason, of sanity, of peace that the premier ever got to hear, "for more and more upheavals. This is just the beginning. For once men taste even the smallest bite of freedom, like the wolf and its first lick of blood, they long for more. Must have more above all else. It is within your destiny to strengthen that freedom, to make the world strong enough to fight Killov and future Killovs, of whom there will always be more. Then you can die, Grandfather, in peace — knowing you have done the right thing and that the torch of life burns brighter. You can die smiling, Grandfather — it is still within your power."

"My head, my head, it hurts," Vassily cried out, slumping back in his wheelchair, his face turning white, blue veins sticking out like webbing around the crinkled face. "Please, no more words, not tonight. They cut like blades, they hurt."

"Grandfather, grandfather," Rahallah whispered sadly, shaking his head from side to side. The man was going to pieces. He slowly wheeled the premier back through the wide glass doors to his bedroom and lifted him like a ragdoll from the chair, depositing him as tenderly as a father a child in the center of the soft down feather bed.

"Yes, sleep. Thank you, Faithful One. Go now, eat. Leave me. Let this old man drift into blackness where there is no thought, where I can hide from the grins of the skulls that circle me like vultures above carrion. Let me sleep, Rahallah, and do not wake me unless the earth is about to be destroyed."

"Yes, Grandfather," the black servant answered, backing off from the world's leader and shutting the door to the main hall softly behind him.

"No one, absolutely no one but me is to disturb him," Rahallah ordered the two Elite Guards who stood in front of the doorway, armed with smgs and body plates.

"Sir!" both of them barked back, clicking their boots together sharply. They hated having to take commands from the black man, but until Vassily died, the African slave was the second most powerful man in the world. After Vassily died, the man would be dog-meat!

Rahallah headed down the hall to his room, shutting the door and locking it behind him as prying eyes were everywhere. Dark forces seemed to fill the air like the thick pressure before a rainstorm.

Rahallah, the Son-of-the-Plains-Lion, stripped off the tuxedo, the clothing of the white man, until he stood naked in the center of his luxurious carpeted room. He walked to the closet and pulled out a large burlap bag filled to the bursting point, and extracted the sacred ceremonial clothes one by one and put them on. The leopard-skin loincloth, then the witch doctor's hat, his father's legacy, passed through the generations along with all the magical lore of the Imbagi tribe of Kenya. With hands as slow and careful as a bomb expert defusing a thousand-pounder, Rahallah placed the triangular hat made of a lion's mane on his head. Then he put a necklace made of the lion's teeth—shining like a hundred magic tusks—around his neck. He took a tiny bag of powder and walked out to his own private terrace where no one could see him and knelt down on the cold stone.

The snow coated him quickly with a sugary frosting, but he felt nothing. Neither pleasure nor pain. He took a pinch of the brown dust from the medicine bag and built a little pile of the crumbling substance just in front of his knees. With a small flint striker he ignited it while murmuring a chant, and the powder caught, burning instantly white hot but without flame. A powerful odor of the African sacred herb filled his nostrils as the smoke wafted up, surrounding his head. He reached into the burlap bag for the final things he needed and pulled out a stick with numerous weathered ivory skulls of small plains creatures hanging down from it, bumping together as he moved. Rahallah raised his arms to the sky, opening them wide, shaking the skull-stick.

"Oh Gods of the Plain, Gods of the Fire,
Hear my voice as Prince of the Lions,
Reach to me all the way from the Serengeti,
from the Rift Valley.
Fill the mind of the Grandfather with peace,
with freedom.
Only your powers can stop the darkness from
falling.
Hear me! Hear me! Hear me! Or I will desert
you,
And I am your only believer!

Rahallah didn't pray for help—he demanded it,
shaking the skull-stick at the writhing gray clouds
above, which continued to send down curtains of the
fluffy thick flakes of snow. The whiteness quickly
covered him, so that only his arms and mouth, which
continued to move in ritual motion, were visible.
Through the long night he vocalized the ancient
words, the secret harmonies to call up the gods of
Africa, to make them rise right up through the
parched earth of the plains, make them fly down
from the icy perches of Mt. Kilimanjaro. For the way
things were going—no human was going to save the
rad-sickened planet. Only the ancient gods, if they
cared any longer.

Chapter Eight

"I love your nails," Rona smirked sarcastically from atop her loping 'brid to Kim, who rode just yards away. "You must tell me who does them."

"No one does them," the president's blond-haired, blue-eyed daughter smiled back icily. "They're beautiful naturally—just like every other part of me. But I hear you're having a lot of trouble with your own 'natural' attributes—things starting to sag and wrinkle. I know a plastic surgeon in a cave outside of Topeka who can do wonders with—well, anyone—even you."

"How kind," Rona said, forcing down the bile rising in her stomach once again, repressing the urge to smash the smaller woman in the face with a nose-crushing karate blow. "I see he's done wonders for you. No beauty, of course—but then look what he had to work with. But cute—yes, quite cute. From a sow's ear into—"

Rockson rode several yards ahead of the bickering pair, trying to keep his ears locked closed so he wouldn't have to listen. They had both demanded to be taken with the Doomsday Warrior on the mission. One, maybe—but Rock knew that there was no way in hell he was going to be able to argue both of them out of it, so he simply surrendered. But by the first few hours out it was clear that a continuous stream of highly acidic conversation between the two was going to be the order of the day.

After the gathered military delegates back in Century City had voted to follow Rockson's plan, the fortresses to be attacked were assigned to different cities—pretty much according to their manpower, their armaments, their ability to take on a particular-sized Russian fort. Century City's top battle strategists gave suggestions to those who were willing to listen on the best mode of attack and the time was set. Fourteen days. They would return to their towns and cities and assemble every bit of man *and* woman power they could. At the same hour in fourteen days, the free forces would strike across America in a coordinated attack. And like D-Day almost 150 years ago—everything was riding on it.

Rockson led a smaller elite unit of Century City's forces, his own team of Chen, Detroit, Archer, and McCaughlin and ten other hand-picked men. And of course, Kim and Rona, who were giving the rest of the team their fair share of laughs. They would link up with the much larger—nearly 5,000-man—Century City army at Fort Minsk. It was the largest of the midwest fortresses, the central headquarters of military operations for the entire KGB takeover, and if their intel reports were correct—the place that Killov had fled to after miraculously surviving the Octagon's explosion in Washington. Rockson felt the takeover of Minsk was essential to the success of the war. If they could take out the brain—the arms, the legs would fail. If not . . . But failure was not something Ted Rockson dwelled on. If he did, he would have given up long ago and crawled back into the radioactive dirt. For everything is impossible until you do it.

"Tell me," Kim said, not even deigning to look at her opponent in love, "how *did* you get that red hair? Mecco-root?"

"Darling—it's all my own—as is everything you see," Rona replied with an absurd little laugh. "It's a pity there's so little to see on you."

"Men just love little packages, dear," Kim retorted, throwing a hand over her mouth in a little yawn as if the entire proceeding was getting most tedious. "It makes them feel so manly. With you, I would think it would be more along the lines of a wrestling match or a weight-lifting competition—and I'm sure you would do very well."

Paces ahead, Rockson didn't know whether to laugh or cry. Men always said they liked that kind of problem—two beautiful women in love with you at the same time. But in reality, it was a different matter. For they spent so much time arguing, there was no energy left for him. But at least they weren't pulling at each other's hair and scratching at one another's eyes.

He loved them both, each in a different way, each bringing up a whole different range of emotions. He had been Rona's only lover for years. Though she knew that he slept with others along the road from time to time, she had never made an issue of it. A man is a man is a man. As long as no little hussy from Century City made a stab at *her* man. And none dared—not against the 5'10", 140 pounds of pure muscle and fighting ability of Rona Wallender. Descended from a famous circus-trapeze family, Rona had been trained as a child in gymnastics and acrobatics, working as a performer in her father's traveling show—secretly an intelligence-gathering operation for the Freefighters. When her father was captured and executed, Rona had managed to escape and made her way to Century City. The rest was history. She and Rockson had hooked up, and . . . Until Kim showed up, she had been his woman.

The two women were as different from one another as the sun and the moon. Green-eyed Rona—tall, strong, strikingly deep tanned, long-legged, with a face of chiseled beauty, and a mane of flaming red hair that cascaded down her back like a waterfall. She was a star-patterned mutant, too—like Rockson. Strong, tough as nails, resistant to radiation and a host of diseases. And in bed she had taken Rockson to heights of passion even he hadn't dreamed existed.

Kim was everything Rona was not—petite at 5'2", blonde, alabaster-complexion, a little on the shy side. She was the all-American girl and, had she lived a hundred years before, would surely have been a model, with a near-perfect look of a certain type of girl who existed only here in the USA. It wasn't really that she was striking in any way, and if her features were looked at one at a time—ivory skin with a few freckles, blue-green eyes, almost pug nose—she wouldn't have seemed all that special. But somehow when they were all put together as a face—there was a remarkable open soft beauty that Rockson had found irresistible.

The Doomsday Warrior decided to just sit back in the saddle and enjoy it. At least he wouldn't have to choose between the two—not while they were both hammering away at each other's psyches like two boxers jabbing, constantly jabbing, looking for the slightest weakness so they could come in for the knockout blow.

"How do you take care of yourself when you're on your own?" Rona asked Kim with mock concern. "I mean, when there are no men around for you to be protected by?"

"Oh, haven't I shown you my arsenal?" Kim laughed. "I'm loaded for bear, darling." She flung open her velcron-layered field jacket to reveal two pearl-handled .45's strapped to her waist, a set of throwing knives ready for quick draw, and a snub-nosed magna/aluminum Ingram with a 30-slug clip. "When there's trouble—it's usually the men who come to me," the petite blonde said coolly. And so it went, the rest of the team silent, as they all rode along in single file. Only the barbs of the young women passed back and forth like little platters of poison punctuated the air. Each thought: When we bed down, *I* will be with *him*.

They rode for hours into the evening and then the night, which grew dark as heavy storm clouds migrated by above heading east to deposit their straining loads. Rock decided to camp about midnight, sensing that Snorter, his 'brid, was beginning to falter. And if that giant among mutant horses was feeling tired, the others were surely ready to drop.

He held his right hand straight up and cried out,

"Rest stop—six hours!" The 15 man, 2 woman team headed the 'brids about fifty yards over to a grove of jungle-leaved willow trees, their nuke-mutated hanging branches forming a protective canopy from the elements and from prying Red spy drones in the morning sky—although since the KGB had attempted its coup, Rockson realized that he had seen not one of the cigar-shaped unmanned camera-rockets flying by. Out of the worst of occurrences came useful results.

The 'brids were given their nylon bags filled with high-protein oats and then allowed to graze on tender morsels nearby while the men set up their sleeping bags and undid their tents, just in case the pack of thunderheads riding miles above their heads should decide to spill out their guts of rain water. McCaughlin quickly set up his mini-kitchen, pulling supplies, pots, and pans down from his two pack 'brids. Using smokeless, low-light flame pellets, he cooked up a meal of rabbit and carrot stew, whose odors had every Freefighter in camp lined up with plate in hand before the tough meat had had time to soften.

"Just wait, pull your belts tighter around your stomachs," the big-bellied Scottish fighter/chef said, waving a long stainless-steel ladle at them. "You eat rabbit before it's tender as a chicken and you won't be getting much sleep tonight. Not with said rabbit trying to jump through your intestinal tract and back up to its burrow."

At last the food was ready and the Freefighters sat around in a circle eating, swapping crude insults, although the level of the joking didn't slip quite to the usual depths since there were "ladies" present. Thankfully, Kim and Rona kept quiet as they ate, realizing that everyone had probably had about enough for the day. But as Rockson finished and went to turn in after posting guards, both women followed him, setting up their own sleeping sacks on each side of him just yards away. All three of them lay there unable to really fall asleep as they felt the emotions run between them like electric current through a wire. They lay on their backs, eyes open, looking straight up at the sky, each with his or her own seething thoughts and desires. Suddenly the night lit up above as several meteors flew down into the lower atmosphere, burning up in gigantic bonfires in the sky. Since the war, the lower levels of atmosphere in the biospheres around the earth had allowed debris from space to burn more slowly, sometimes hitting the ground in somewhat larger chunks than it had in the past. And the larger masses burned spectacularly at lower altitudes as they speeded up, pulled down by the clutching arms of gravity. The sky was suddenly filled with balls of fire, screaming down from their trillion-mile journeys through space. The meteorites were so large that the Freefighters could see the shapes of them as they came burning down like hawks with their wings on fire, swooping in at stark angles. A globe of white seemed to drop right down on them, filling the night sky with near-daylight for a second. Then it whooshed past, crashing several miles off. They could see the explosion, the white glow filling the horizon for a moment. Rona's and Kim's hearts were beating like pistons, but neither made a sound or reached out to be held by the man they loved. They were like two wolves circling prey, each waiting for the other to make a move. Rockson, seeing no alternative, glumly slept alone.

The next day, Rockson woke them all early and after freeing the 'brids from their daily collection of burrs, brambles, and twigs, the force loaded up and was off again. Kim and Rona got on the case again within minutes of striking the trail.

"You look like you could have used a few more hours of beauty sleep," Kim said, looking over at Rona, whose eyes were often puffy when she first woke up.

"At least I have something to beautify, dear one," Rona replied, sitting high in the saddle, her khaki field jacket wide open in the morning heat, revealing her large melon breasts pushing against her gray sweat shirt.

"Something's not the word, darling," Kim went on without missing a beat. "I would say stockpile is more accurate."

"If a man came to you looking for supplies," Rona spat out, "I daresay he'd find only empty shelves." And so it went.

The attack force rode for hours, the clouds dissipating as the sun rose higher, cutting them apart with its golden machinegun rays. They came to a rise in the increasingly sparsely vegetated terrain and Rockson took his field glasses to scan ahead. A motion on the ground several hundred yards forward caught his eyes. A long undulating shape, thick as a branch. A snake—a big one. As he moved the glasses to the right he saw another, then another.

"Judas Priest," the Doomsday Warrior cried out,

causing Rona and Kim, sitting atop their 'brids on either side of him, to take out their own binocs and look.

"Yech," Kim said, making a disgusted expression. "They're everywhere, Rock—it looks like hundreds of them spread out all across the near part of the plain."

"Scared of a few snakes, dear?" Rona shot out, seeing her chance.

"It *is* silly, isn't it?" Kim answered instantly. "With such a large target as you—why would they ever go after me?"

Rockson looked left and right as far as he could see and then turned to the rest of the men who had come to a stop behind him.

"I'm afraid we're going to have to go through them. Must be some sort of breeding grounds—extends for miles. We can't play around trying to detour."

"But Rock," Rona said, suddenly feeling not a little squeamish herself. "Surely some of them are poisonous—how—how will we get through? I mean, the 'brids—" She stuttered on, nearly incomprehensible, as she slowly realized that he really meant it.

"We can use the new aluma-tarps that Dr. Shecter developed. His tech boys reformulated them so they can be split into strips and used for other purposes. They're as strong as steel, flexible—just perfect for hybrid armor."

It took them almost half an hour to get the wide protective tarpaulins—based on the space blanket of the 20th century—wrapped around the legs of their 'brids from the hoof to top of the thigh and secured with tape. The animals didn't seem to like the idea too much, making noises to that effect—but they had

107

been well trained back in Century City and allowed themselves to be girded. When the Freefighters finished and stood back to see what they had wrought, they had to squelch the laughs. For the creatures looked like overstuffed, badly made carousel horses, walking around stiffly from the somewhat confining pieces of aluma-tarp. But beauty was not the name of the game out in the wastelands of post-nuke America. Only their hoofs and eyes were uncovered.

Rockson ordered the team to mount up—and pull their legs up onto their 'brids' shoulders out of reach of the acres of snakes. Slowly, every man in the unit, even Rockson himself, feeling the deep unconscious fear of the man's most ancient enemy—the serpent— deep in his guts, started down the pebble-strewn slope toward the plain below. The 'brids grew increasingly nervous as they approached the gauntlet of living venom-tubes, raising their heads high and looking down out of the wide fear-opened eyes. Rock hoped that the snakes would just let them pass, not wanting to get trampled by the large 'brids. But such was not to be.

The moment Rock's hybrid reached the start of the obstacle course, the snakes went wild. It was as if they had been waiting just for this moment to arrive. As if with one mind, one living body with a hundred thousand tentacles, the plains all around them came to life in a slithering of slimy bodies. There were snakes of every size and color, thick black ones like eels with their dark mouths open and hissing, green and red ones, moving like slashes of electric color across the light brown dirt. From little worms the size of pencils with fangs nearly as large as their bodies to pythons twenty feet long with jaws opening like a shark's ready to swallow a man whole — and maybe try a second course of hybrid horse. And they were all coming in one direction. If there is a universal human phobia, it is that of snakes. What man can look upon the face of a viper, stare into those diamond eyes as orange as the back side of the sun, and not fear that forked tongue flicking in and out, endlessly tasting the scent of evil in the air? Who can look and not know that that face is descended from Eden's demon?

"Rock, Rock!" Kim screamed just behind the Doomsday Warrior as her 'brid reared up, nearly toppling her from the saddle. Her boots had come out of the stirrups.

"Hold on, Kim. Wrap your legs around its neck, grip the saddle horn with both arms." There was no stopping, no time for mistakes. The snakes closed in from all sides like the twin walls of the Red Sea crashing together against the terrified riders and their mounts. They leapt and struck out with jaws agape as if they were ready to swallow the world. Thousands of pairs of fangs closed on the aluma-tarps around the hybrids' legs, searching for flesh in which to inject their venoms — poisons which could take out even a 'brid in a matter of seconds. But the death-dripping hypodermics couldn't penetrate the material. An ooze of venom began running down the sides of the 'brids' legs. The 'brids stepped high — and fast, scrunching many.

Rockson knew it couldn't go on like this for long — one of them would get up high enough to reach paydirt, and . . . He leaned around in his saddle and screamed out over the disquieting sound of ten thousand snapping rubbery jaws, "Hit the 'brids! Scream at 'em—shoot your pistols off next to their heads—make 'em more scared of you than the snakes!" The men did as Rockson ordered, kicking, yelling in the ears of the animals. Guns went off, firing in the air as the snakes continued their ceaseless barrage against the foil-covered legs of the panic-stricken steeds. When an animal is frightened, the only way to regain control of it is to take back control of its mind—be a more powerful fear-force than the one confronting it. Or so the theory goes. And in this case it worked. The pistol shots terrified the 'brids, who had been running in circles into one another, stepping high, afraid to venture further out into the sea of living serpents. The barks of the guns, the men screaming as if kingdom come had come, panicked them into a dead-ahead galloping stampeded. Rockson took the lead with Snorter and shot across the moving ground as the other 'brids closed rank behind, all of them running as fast as their steel girded legs could carry them.

Thousands of the snakes were trampled, ground into bloody mud beneath the 'brids' pulverizing hooves. Yet still the serpents on every side flew into the air as the 'brids approached, trying to judge their airborne trajectory so as to reach the faces of the tearing animals or the things that rode atop them. The Freefighters kept shooting on every side of them, firing first one way then the other and reloading with snap-in clips in seconds. The streaks of black and gray erupted in explosive blasts of snakeskin and innards as the .45 cal., 7mm and 9mm, along with Rock's own .12 gauge death-presents all turned the air around them into putrid mists of red.

God only knew how many vipers they sent back to hell, but the Freefighters weren't counting—just killing. The stampede went on with no intention of stopping—only the sheer speed and power of the large mammals and the leg armoring allowed them to slam their way through what, for any other creature on earth—even a three-horn grizzly—meant certain paralyzing death. Rock heard a piercing scream behind him even above the constant gunfire and turned around to see one of the new men picked for the mission, sandy haired Matheson, wrestling with a four-foot-long piece of writhing death. The black snake with four yellow and red stripes running parallel down the sides of its body had its fangs sunk full-length into the man's neck and was pumping out grams of nerve poison. Matheson managed to rip the thing out and heave it away and back down to the writhing army below. He threw his hands around his throat and his whole head seemed to lift up, his neck stretching impossibly long. Then his entire body began spasming, the arms and legs jerking out of control. The body tumbled from the saddle and down to the sea of death. In a second it was covered with a blanket of the things. The others had to go on. They rode for minutes that seemed like days, but at last the snakes seemed to grow less dense and then they were gone completely. Rockson made them ride on for another thirty seconds to make sure the wretched creatures wouldn't come after them, and then pulled Snorter to a stop. The other 'brids, their energy gone in the mad burst and seeing no more of the squirming things crawling around their ankles, also slowed and halted, their foam-flecked jaws hanging open from the exertion, their tongues hanging out panting like dogs.

"Everyone still here?" Rock asked, making a quick head count.

"Everyone except Matheson, poor bastard," said McCaughlin, who had been taking the rear, spitting out a disgusted wad onto the dirt below.

"At least he didn't suffer," added Chen, who had been riding just behind the unfortunate man. "I saw him go down—he was dead before he hit the ground. That poison was like a cyanide injection to the brain."

"Anyone else? Any 'brids acting funny?" Rock asked. They all looked around at themselves and each other—and somehow nothing was the worse for wear. Matheson's hybrid, who had followed the orders, stood looking up at Rockson nervously as if it had done something wrong.

"McCaughlin, take that extra 'brid and hook him up with your kitchen team. Might need him later. And don't, whatever any of you do, touch the aluma-tarps! They're covered with the stuff—you can see it like syrup coating the outer surface. We'll have to be careful until we reach a stream where we can wash the stuff off. So don't let your legs down, or your hands rub against it, okay?"

He didn't have to worry. After experiencing the ocean of demonic creatures, none of them was going to mess around with the excretions. As uncomfortable as their legs were in the muscle-straining position high on their mounts' backs, they tried to hold them even higher to avoid being anywhere near the moist, poisonous deposits.

"East—we'll keep due east," Rock said, starting Snorter forward at a slow gait. "I know this area, there's a river ahead a few miles." They followed behind slowly like a funeral procession. Even Kim and Rona were at a complete loss for words, their hearts still beating so rapidly that they felt as if they would crack their ribcages. Both were deeply shaken—but neither wanted to admit it. So they rode with heads hung down as if in mourning for the lost Matheson.

Unlike snakes of the pre-nuke war era, which had but two fangs and swallowed their prey whole, the post-war monstrosities that Rockson and his team had barely survived had *rows* of inward-curving teeth about a quarter-inch long. This enabled them to actually chew off pieces of their victims, rather than having to eat them all at once or have nothing at all. Times were hard. Only those creatures, those species that had adapted and continued to adapt to the rapidly changing environments of the earth, would survive.

Thus Matheson's body was shared by hundreds of the undulating serpents, who ripped the carcass apart like lions at a feed. They sank their jaws deep into the bloody flesh, locked them like clamps, and then pulled back with all their weight, ripping pieces right out. The epidermis and layers of muscle were consumed within minutes. Some of the smaller vipers slid inside the body through the nose and mouth and eaten-out eye sockets. Down through the throat and the intestines they slithered, ripping at the membranous walls around them until at last they bit through to the treasures their kind thirsted after above all else—the inner organs. These they dug into with wild abandon, biting and snapping around until their bodies were coated from snout to tail with blood. They ate for hours in this warm dream sea of consumable flesh.

Chapter Nine

"You see anyone?" Rockson asked the men crouching in the dark on each side of him as they slowly scanned the Red radio-relay outpost with their binocs from a nearby hill.

"Nothing," Chen whispered back. "The gates closed."

"Zip," said Detroit, letting the mini-glasses fall back around his chest and taking up 2 grenades in his grit-coated strong black hands.

"Then, it's a go," Rock whispered as he motioned forward with his arm twice, signaling the rest of the Freefighting force waiting behind him in the bushes. With the passage of Rockson's plan of attack back in Century City, the Doomsday Warrior had taken that as a mandate to mean *all* of his plan. Including that part about trying to strike a deal with Premier Vassily. And that meant talking with the man, or at least with his aide-de-camp, Rahallah, who had some say in the Kremlin.

The small Red Army outpost that the Freefighters were edging toward was a long-distance communications outpost whose function was to intercept radio messages from other Red fortresses for a distance of up to 1,000 miles and relay them by satellite back to Moscow's central Army headquarters. There they'd be pumped into their Decode-Computer. If Rock could get hold of the sophisticated transmission gear locked away in the concrete bunker — and get one of the technicians to operate it — he might have a shot at getting through. But the best-laid plans of mice and mutants . . .

They had barely gotten past the surrounding barbed wire perimeter, slicing through it with mini-wirecutters — one of many small tools that Mc-Caughlin carried on the supply 'brids' backs — when a floodlight swooped down and caught the three lead Freefighters frozen for a split second in mid-stride.

"Take 'em out," Rockson yelled above the momentary silence, as the Reds slowly realized that someone was attacking them — the first time in the ten years the base had been there. Without giving them a chance to organize, the Freefighters swarmed out of the darkness, their Liberators set on full auto, firing sprays of 9mm slugs at every dark uniform they saw.

The gunners in the two machine-gun emplacements on each side of the forty-yard-wide outpost frantically swung their big .50 cals. around on their tripods, trying to sight up the fighters who jumped and darted like grasshoppers, impossible to follow through the lenses. Suddenly from out of the midst of the attackers came two spinning steel pineapples. In each tower the guards scrambled toward the wooden stairs, letting their ammo belts drop to the floor. But not one made it as the grenades Detroit had flung detonated with fiery roars. Red bodies flew through the sky, clothing blazing like sizzling comets, filling the night with the stench of human flesh.

It's an ancient adage — probably going back to the first Neanderthal's invasion of his neighbor's cave — but *surprise* is the most powerful ally a fighting force can have. The enemy is caught off guard, asleep, taking a piss out back. And in the vital seconds it takes just to comprehend what's going on — it's too late. The Freefighters threw their ropes, climbed the walls and swept through the compound with the ferocity and timing of a pack of tigers, destroying with claws of burning slugs every Russian stupid or slow enough to stay in range. Rockson's fifteen-man team was probably the best-trained, toughest unit in Century City — and thus in the entire country. The poor bastards didn't have a chance. Even Rona and Kim were taking their toll, from the hill, with long range IR-scoped shots. Rock and Chen headed for the main concrete bunker set dead center of the base, dodging a line of machine-gun fire that was tracing closer to them by the second.

"Down, boys, down," the deep voice of Detroit Green bellowed out just behind them. They hit the ground as another pair of Freefighter presents wrapped in sweat came tearing over their heads. The Red gunner tried to sight up the nearly indistinguishable black man, squinting through the eight-inch-wide slit in his pillbox about seventy feet ahead. Detroit was not just a grenade thrower — he was the ace grenade thrower. Back in Century City, he was the eternal star of the military baseball team, which played the civvies twice a year. The long muscular arms on his squat muscular body could generate such power and pinpoint accuracy that neither the opposing baseball team nor the Commies stood a chance. Both of Detroit's death apples flew through the narrow opening, one hitting the machine gunner on the side of the head. He nearly blacked out, came to in about a second, and looked down to see the two globes lying motionless on the floor as if waiting to be picked up. He had just enough time to turn and reach for the door, his fingers barely touching the knob, when they both went off. What was left of him slid underneath the door, making a belated gelatin-like exit from the charnel room.

"Go! Go!" Rock yelled, seeing the smoke pour out of the sighting slot. They charged forward, eyes darting back and forth through the smoke and the tracers. The Freefighters pounded through panicked groups of half-naked men who came charging from their sleeping quarters, screaming in terror and firing wildly in every direction—half the shots hitting their own men. Rock's men just hit the dirt and opened up at waist level, mowing them down like beer bottles on a rickety fence. Only these bottles spouted brews of blood when hit.

Rockson hit the stairs that led to a steel door about ten feet below a pillbox.

"Crack it," he yelled out to Detroit, who ripped two more high-explosive doughnuts from the ammo belts crisscrossed over his chest.

"Concussion, Rock," Detroit screamed above the battle, "gonna make a pow." He placed the grenades against each side of his mouth, ripped the pins out with his teeth, and let them drop down the stairs, bouncing along like metal tennis balls. Rock, Chen, and Detroit flew backward through the air and hit the ground, hugging the dirt as if it were a willing woman. Suddenly they were lost in a thunderous roar and were blanketed with chunks and particles of dirt and concrete. Before the noise had stopped reverberating in their eardrums, they were up and heading down the smoky stairs, weapons out, nerves on hair trigger. The concussion had lifted the three-inch-thick steel door right out of its frame and sent it flying backward, apparently crushing someone who had been standing just behind it into a pulp that oozed out from underneath it.

Rockson was praying that the Russians had followed their typical course when building the communications outpost. As was the way of the Russian Empire—everything planned. Everything came down from the top, from bureaucrats who sat around in huge empty halls making plans and forms for the world. In Century City, the Doomsday Warrior had taken the opportunity to go through captured Russian books and letters whenever they were taken along with the other booty. And he knew they always built the com units dead center of the subbasement, reasoning that it was the most protected place in case of full-scale artillery attack—though where the Freefighters were going to get any nuclear weapons had apparently never crossed their minds.

The three Rock Team Freefighters, their faces red with exertion, sweatshirts drenched with sweat, tore through the basement searching for the stairs to the lowest level.

Rockson suddenly felt himself slammed aside by Chen, a burst of .50 cal smg fire missing his head by inches. The Chinese Freefighter martial-arts master used the collision against Rock's body to throw himself off in the other direction. While in motion, he flung two five-pointed *shuriken* from under his sleeve and then hit the other wall, sinking to the floor in an instant. The advancing Russian gunner kept firing, spraying the weapon back and forth down the hall—until the first spinning blade caught him just under the Adam's apple. It cut three inches into the man's throat, severing everything of any importance along the way. The Red dropped his rifle and slammed both palms over his sudden uninvited throat operation as if trying to keep everything from falling out. But it fell out—in a gush of blood and vomit—and the man fell to the concrete spasming in his own red liquid, his eyes already fixed and staring.

"Sorry for the push, Rock," Chen said as the three men rose to their feet and started forward again. "Didn't think you wanted to make that fellow's acquaintance."

"He's not my type," the Doomsday Warrior muttered as he started forward into near darkness, his .12 gauge shotpistol cocked near his head. He saw just a glint of light on the floor—then it was gone. Rock dropped to his knees, lowered his head to the cold cement, and began squinting furiously. Chen and Detroit looked at each other as if their leader had gone mad.

"Uh, lose a contact lens or something?" Detroit asked, holding another grenade in his right hand and his chromium .45 in the other.

"I saw a glint—I think—I think. Here!" he said excitedly. "This is it. A trap door down to the next level. It's sealed tight — but not tight enough. What do you think?" he asked Detroit as he traced the barely noticeable edges of the pseudo-concrete door below with his fingertips.

"Got enough apples with me — but that's it," Detroit said, hitting the floor with a fist. "Feels thick, Rock. These Reds — sometimes they built 'em two feet, three feet thick. These might not do shit against that — but we'll see." He took the remaining six grenades from his web belt — the rest were back with his 'brid — and placed them around the perimeter of the sealed door. Instead of pulling the pins, Detroit flicked a small lever on the mini-bombs that switched on their radio detonation controls. Rock shouted to the other men to mop up and stay alert, while his team went into the bunker.

"All right," the black bull of a man said, standing up. "Let's find a place to hide — and — we'll see." Detroit sounded a little edgy as if not quite sure that the grenades were really capable of doing the job. And since he was the explosives-man on the team, he felt that the success or failure of the mission was on his head. They headed back around a cement wall and Detroit pulled a small transmitter from a pouch on his belt.

"Close your eyes and cover your ears, boys and girls," the dust-covered Freefighter said with a smirk. " 'Cause it's party time." He turned a lever on the cigarette pack-sized transmitter and a roar filled the floor they were standing on. A shock wave followed instantaneously and the three of them were thrown from their feet and covered with a blanket of debris from the detonation. "Hey," Chen whispered, "kill

121

them, not *us*."

Detroit was the first one up and around the corner—wanting to see with his own eyes whether it had worked. He shot forward, trying to peer through the still-swirling smoke—and then saw it. The grenades had blasted the concealed hatch right out of the floor. He could see down into a large chamber below, filled with dust and voices yelling in terror.

"Don't kill 'em if you can help it," Rock yelled out as Detroit prepared to swing down. "We need at least one tech expert alive—otherwise, we've just wasted a lot of ammo."

"To hear is to obey, Effendi," Detroit said, disappearing down into the steaming hole, followed by Rockson and then Chen. As they swung into the communications center, hanging onto the sides of the opening and then dropping the two yards to the hard floor, the stunned, dust covered Russian techs around the hundred-foot-square room ran around like chickens with their heads cut off. They weren't fighters—just communications specialists and repairmen whose training was in turning dials, not pulling triggers. They didn't want to die—and from the looks of the filth-covered American rebels who were coming after them, it appeared that that was the general idea.

Several of them tore over to the guncase—it was impossibly cumbersome for them to carry their weapons while working with the transmission equipment—and grabbed for pistols, Kalashnikovs—anything their hands touched. The first to arm themselves turned and tried to draw a bead on the weaving American fighters, who had just dropped in.

"Don't shoot," Rock screamed out. "No one down here has to die if you do what we tell you. I promise you as an officer of the Re-United States Army." Several of the more ambitious young techs saw their chance to make a name for themselves by killing the attackers and continued to sight up the Americans, squeezing off shots that missed their furtive targets by a mile. Rockson dove forward on the floor and somersaulted over twice, coming up in a crouch. He fired his .12 gauge pistol three times and the three Russian techs who'd had ideas of being heroes tumbled to the floor behind a long workbench covered with soldering equipment, their weapons flying from their hands, blood pouring out of the wide wounds that shotgun shells make.

"Over here, bastard," a voice suddenly yelled with a thick Russian accent. Rock turned to see a large beer-bellied military officer, possibly the overseer of the technical team, holding an arm around Chen's neck, a Turganev revolver poised against his head. "Anyone moves," he said, in passably understandable English, "and your little buddy here gets his brains sent back down to China." Rock and Detroit froze, their pistols useless as the Red was using the Chinese American as a shield.

But not for long. At the instant the Russian said the word "China," Chen was in motion. His left hand whipped up with the blurred speed of a propeller, knocking the pistol into the air, while the other hand reached down and behind him, slamming into the Russian's groin with the force of a mule kick. The big man didn't even have time to scream out in agony as the diminutive martial arts master turned and, mak-

123

ing spear fingers with both hands, drove them into the Russian's ears. The stiff fingers sank in nearly four inches, digging clear into his brain. Chen pulled them out in a flash, followed by a sludgy mess of pink that poured out from the ruptured skull cavity. The Russian stood stock still for a moment, a look of horrified surprise frozen on his face, and then he toppled forward, splattering the floor with what had been his mind. Chen wiped his sticky fingers clean on his pants and turned, ready for whoever else wanted to buy tickets into the next life.

But there were no more takers. The remaining dozen techs lay cowering behind tables and consoles as the room beeped and clicked with a billion rubles worth of high-tech equipment.

"Okay, everybody up," Rockson said, motioning with his shotpistol. As they were slow to rise, he fired once into the ceiling and the Reds sprang to their feet, their hands raised high in the air. "We're not here to waste all of you," Rock said softly, trying to calm the white-faced radio operatives with a soothing tone. "You do what I want—and you'll all live, all get to take your wives and little babushkas rowing on the Volga again. Anyone *else* speak a little Ameri-kansky?"

"I—I know you," one of the techs stuttered, his eyes growing even wider in alarm. "I've seen your picture. That white streak of hair down the center of your scalp: one blue, one violet eye. It's you! You—you're *the Rockson*—the head of the rebels. They say you love nothing more than to cut off heads—and—put them on a stake." The man looked as if he were about to lose his dinner. "We are dead men," he said resignedly.

"Appreciate the notoriety," Rockson smiled back. "But I'm not giving autographs today—and not taking any heads. All we want and need is telecom linkup to the Kremlin. I want to talk to your Premier Vassily." Rock couldn't help but grin as he watched the faces of the technicians grow a whiter shade of pale.

"They will know it was *us*," one of the Russians whispered out in his own language through clamped vocal cords. "They'll kill us. Put us on the dissident's crucifixes outside Moscow, if we do as he says."

Rockson, who understood a smattering of Russian interjected, "Pal, when I get finished talking to the Great One, they'll give you all the Medal of Lenin. Now listen to me—shake some sense into those propaganda-filled things you call heads," the Doomsday Warrior said, letting his gun hang down at his side as he walked among the prisoners. Chen and Detroit kept a careful watch from each side, ready to blast anyone who tried anything into a detour to hell.

"Now, me and my buddies here," Rock went on softly, knowing that you can neutralize at least half of a man's fear just by the tone and volume of your voice, "aren't about to slice any heads. You all know what's going on—the KGB has taken all your Red Army chums prisoner—those that it didn't slaughter outright. What the hell do you think they're going to do after they catch up with you?" The technicians who understood looked at one another nervously— for they had been wondering and talking about that very possibility when the door above them had crashed down in pieces.

"What—what do you want us to do?" asked one of the techs, skinny as a stringbean, his face covered with a battlefield of pimples. He was barely out of his teens, he probably wanted to reach 25.

"Just put me in *voice* communications with Vassily—that's all. Anyway, fellows," Rock went on, letting his voice rise a little, putting a tone of coldness into it, "I'm not asking—I'm telling you. We haven't got time." To add a little drama to the words, the Doomsday Warrior whipped his arm up and let loose a shot from his pistol, just missing the skinny tech by inches and blasting the side of the table behind him into splinters.

"I—I'll help you," the pimply young technician shrieked, his voice rising all the way into the higher registers. Several of the others looked at him with scorn but three more joined in a chorus of agreement, yesses and *Da's*.

Within minutes the four Russians sat in front of their radio transmission stations—the rest were locked in a storage closet for safekeeping—madly twisting dials this way and that, as monitors and grid screens lit up with an incomprehensible array of diagrams, detailing the relay routes of the telesat linkup. Rock, Chen, and Detroit watched the largest screen, mounted high on one wall, in fascination; it depicted the earth, the bounce satellite hovering above, their location, and the Moscow radar tower. The radiomen did their work quickly and efficiently, lining up the waves of all the different locales so they were in Transmission Mode Symmetry—all hooked up and ready to go.

"I guess—we're ready," the skinny Red said. Rock

realized that although he was the youngest of the bunch, the fellow was apparently the head of the technical unit as he gave orders to the other three and kept looking back at the Command Screen. "The premier, you say? You want to talk to the premier?" He said the words twice as if trying somehow to assimilate the absurdity of the idea. Nobody could just call up the ruler of the world and say hello.

"Yeah—there's only one, right?" Rock responded, standing just behind the head man. "Vassily—I think he lives in the Kremlin. Tell him his old pal Rock wants to chit-chat."

"Yes—I—I can make contact," the Russian said, suddenly seeming a lot less sure about the whole venture now that it was actually about to happen. He handed Rockson a headset with earphone and mouthpiece. The Doomsday Warrior examined it for a few seconds to make sure it wasn't booby-trapped, and then slipped it over his head. He could hear the static swirling and humming through the earpiece as if they were listening to the atonal music of the stratosphere where the COMSAT swung lazily across the night sky.

The technician hit a few more buttons and a row of lights lit up amber just above his head. Then there was a ringing sound. Once, twice, three times. Rock was just wondering if the whole damned planet was going to be lost because the guy wasn't home when the other end clicked and a voice spoke from 9,874 miles away.

"Who is this? I gave orders that no one, absolutely no one, was to call the Grandfather tonight." Rockson recognized Rahalla's *basso sotto* voice.

"This is Ted Rockson, you might remember me? Listen pal, calling long distance, so got to get to the point. I have an offer I want to make to the premier. I know he'll want to talk to me."

"Rockson!" the voice gasped on the other end. "This—is Rahallah, the premier's manservant. Do you remember me—I was present when you were our—guest—at the Kremlin?"

"Yes, I do," the Doomsday Warrior answered, picturing that stark noble statue-like black face. Somehow he had trusted the man. Something in his eyes. "I believe you are a man of peace," Rockson went on, following a hunch, "I believe you are the premier's conscience—the voice that counsels sanity for the world. And I tell you now—let me talk with him. Whatever went on between us in the past is irrelevant. We have a common enemy—an enemy who will take us *all* down with him. You know what I'm talking about, I know you do."

"Yes," Rahallah answered, his voice shot up through space and back down to the center of America in one-sixteenth of a second. "I know. I have prayed that something would happen—that the premier would act swiftly and powerfully. Perhaps, Ted Rockson, you are the God-sent messenger to save this dying world. Yes, I will get the premier. But he is tired, so tired these days. Speak gently with him. Try to persuade him, not bludgeon him. I will tell you something. I am on your side, Rockson. I am not a Communist—it is not my way. But I do counsel the Grandfather. He is not a bad man, just a man trapped by karmic events that would crush most of us to a pulp. He is, in his own way, trying to do what he

128

believes is best. And I think—if you are careful—you *can* get him to help. Be careful, Rockson—it could all ride on this conversation."

"I hear you, pal," Rock said softly. "And if you're ever over this way, drop by Century City, say Rock sent you."

Within a minute Rockson heard another click and then a feeble voice.

The highly educated Grandfather's English was excellent. "Rockson—you bastard—I was told you were dead; I *hoped* you— "

"Ease up, Excellency," Rockson said softly. "We both, in the past, have screwed each other, okay? We both lied, double-dealed, stabbed each other in the back. So on that score we're even." Rockson waited a second to see what the response would be and heard low laughter and then several quick throat-raking coughs.

"You are right, Rockson," the premier spoke up after spitting a gob of bloody phlegm into his purple silk handkerchief, now coated with the dried red splotches. "We *did* both, as you colloquially say, screw each other. And now . . . ?"

"And now, we're going to help each other, Excellency," Rockson said, glad that they'd at least gotten off on the right foot together. "We know who the threat to the planet Earth is. And though you may think I'm a menace and I certainly don't like you—it's not either of us. We've been banging away at each other for decades and things are still standing. It's the Skull, the murderer—Killov. We know he's taken over huge numbers of your Red Army forts—and Zhabnov has fled D.C. So you can't be too happy about

129

recent developments."

"Happy—no," the premier spat back. "But—my arms are tied, at least for a few months. My forces are spread very thin around the world, and—"

"Don't be a fool," Rockson snarled, deciding to take a chance and rile the old fellow a little. "Whoever your troops are battling—in China, Ethiopia, India—it doesn't matter. Killov—Killov is the only one who matters—the others are just dogs pissing in the bushes. Let's help each other. I need you, and—"

"The Empire crumbles, Rockson—you don't understand. It's nationalistic men like you—always attacking my troops, my convoys, blowing up my fortresses. And when they are gone—barbarism, anarchy. The entire human race will fall into the dark ages from which it will never again arise. I am the last buffer between civilization of any kind and total and complete savagery."

For the first time, Rock suddenly and instantly saw how the premier viewed the world. To him, he *was* the last bastion of western civilization—albeit the Slavic, not the Greco-Roman part—he did see himself holding the walls against the hordes; the mutants, the wolves who would devour it all. Trying to save what was left of the books, the computers, the remnants of the old world. In his own way—perhaps the man was heroic in his misguided attempts.

"Excellency, we could get into a debate about this for hours. About how—what appears to you to be barbarism is actually just the patriotism of men around the world wanting to run their own lives and nations. Debate about how, with true freedom there can be no barbarism because each society will make

130

its laws and culture from the bottom, from the heart, not from the top. You must have had a stern father, and wish to be the same to the world!"

Rockson's perfect pegging of the premier threw the old man for a loop. He hadn't realized that anyone could see him that clearly—and it made him feel suddenly terribly vulnerable. He sat in his sweat-soaked bed holding the red phone near his mouth, but was only able to make the movements of his lips—no sounds.

"All right—now you're angry," Rock said, pushing ahead with complete abandon. "But within your anger—listen to me. We—the Freefighters throughout America—are going to attack the Blackshirt forces. We're going to surround fifty of the biggest bases that Killov has managed to gain control of and we're going to risk our lives to save your men. We can't allow Killov to get total control—to get access to the nuclear stockpile. He'll make the U.S. and the world twice as radioactive as it already is from the Big Blow."

That very thought had been giving nightmares to Premier Vassily. The hundred land-based nuke missiles that Red Army forces had hidden around the occupied country. Killov would have a hard time tracking them down, and getting the launch codes. But he would—doubtless he would.

"What do you want, Rockson?" Vassily asked wearily, as if each second of life was a torturous ordeal.

"I want you to get me some tough men, Excellency. Not Red Army, not guys marching in formation with rows of medals. Not Nazis. I know you've got native forces working for you in various parts of the world. Men who have been out there fighting the 'savages' as you call them. Fighting the Muabir in Asia—the Flame of Allah; fighting the Viet Sinh in Vietnam; the Utapas in Nicaragua. I want some of those men, Excellency. Men who can chew trees and knock down walls with their fists. Men who are ready to die." Rockson could picture Vassily's mind making decisions, calculations. Rockson's offer was truly, too good to pass up.

"Yes, yes, I suppose I could let you have some irregulars from a few spots. Rahallah—you are more up to date on the world military situation that I am at the moment," Vassily said, turning his head to the black servant who stood listening anxiously by the bed. "Where might we scrape up some forces—some real forces, not parade troops?"

"India, sir," Rahallah answered instantly. "That's perhaps the one place on earth right now where things are not at the point of exploding. The rebellion of the Hindu army was put down decisively at the Battle of New Delhi just last month. And there's but one reason we did well there, Excellency."

"Yes, yes," the premier answered, waving his hand impatiently.

"The Sikhs, Excellency. A warrior tribe going back to pre-Biblical times. They have always been fighters—it is passed on from father to son like a sacred heritage. They're some of the toughest fighters in the Empire, Excellency. And with the lull over there, there would be somewhere in the neighborhood of 50,000 of them freed up for other duty."

"Yes, yes, I suppose," Vassily mumbled to himself,

trying to keep up with it all. He had been asleep just three minutes before—and now he was being asked to ally with the Free Americans, an enemy his country had been fighting for nearly 150 years.

Rockson pushed further. "Not 'suppose,' Excellency—you *must* send them. You have no choice. For you are a man of destiny, a man who will be remembered as the centuries themselves turn to dust for what you decide right now. You cannot be vilified as the man who allowed the world to fall back into the very dark ages you say you are trying to save us from. You must act now, today. Every second strengthens the murderer's hands. For he stands unopposed in his drugged madness."

"Yes! Yes!" Vassily suddenly screamed out over the phone, with such force that Rock had to pull the earpieces on his headphone away. "Yes, I'll give you those men—though Lenin knows what the result will be. Whether they'll even fight alongside of you—or against you."

"They'll fight with me, Excellency—because you'll tell them to. Because they are your pawns to do with what you wish."

"Ah, I grow so tired," Vassily croaked, his face breaking out into a cold sweat. Just when he thought he would crumble beneath the tonnage of the world—another weight was thrown on. He could feel his heart speeding up, his blood pressure rising, the migraine headache that he had finally suppressed just hours before—coming back with a vengeance.

"Tell me, Rockson—what do you personally get out of all this?" the premier managed to ask, propping himself up on satin pillows, motioning for Rahallah

133

to hand him a glass of medicinal spirits—brandy—to calm him down. The servant poured him but a few sips in an immense crystal snifter, which the ruler of the world downed like a wino on the long ago evaporated Bowery.

"I get *the Skull* out of my way—for good. He disturbs my dreams. I want one thing in return for our help to you."

"*Your* help to *us*!" Vassily began sputtering again. "You just called *me* to help *you*!"

"Yes—but the result of our aid will release your nephew's entire imprisoned army over here. We will be back to the way things were—but at least you will have your forces."

"Yes, yes, it's true," Vassily said grudgingly. "Well, what?"

"I want all the nuclear devices in America removed, never to return. If you want to fight us with your men, your cannons, your jets—then we will fight. But there can be no more nuclear explosions here. The ecological system is hanging by a thread."

It irritated Vassily to no end that many of the things Rockson was saying were thoughts he had had himself in the darkness of his nights. He had read too much, knew too much about the ecosystem not to see the truth. Yet having been the highest of the high for as long as he could remember, it was difficult making deals with a Freefighter mutant who had killed or been responsible for killing literally hundreds of thousands of his men.

"Rockson," Vassily spat out. "You're too damned clever. But as Caesar said to Mark Antony:

'Let me have men about me that are fat;
Sleek-headed men and such as sleep o' nights.
Yon Cassius has a lean and hungry look;
He thinks too much: such men are dangerous.'

"Still, I give my word. I had been thinking of deactivating the missiles anyway, having come to some of the same conclusions as you. But if—and only if—your insane plan works, I'll do it forthwith."

"Sir, I never begin anything I can't finish," Rockson said. "In wine, women—or war."

Within a few more minutes, as the incredulous young Russian radio operator listened in awe, Rockson finished arranging a tentative rendezvous point for Vassily's airlifted troops, to meet their American counterparts.

Chapter Ten

They rode black Arabian stallions, their long white robes flowing like kings' royal garb, their turbans covered with jewels and gold taken from the vanquished, their long curved swords hanging at their sides, ruby-encrusted handles shimmering in the burning noonday sun. They were like visions of some distant past, out of a magical world of genies, dragons, and harems with silk-covered dancing girls. But they lived here in the 21st century. And they killed.

Sikh Pratha Ragdar and Sikh Sinh Panchali—the generals of the Sikh Army that had just won a long, drawn-out fight with the Uttar Pradesh rebel elements. They would rise again, of that both generals were sure—but it would be years. The guerilla movement in India and Pakistan had been seriously hurt with the destruction of half their forces and the capture of their entire top staff—whose heads now sat atop long spikes lining the roads of Northern India like signposts to hell.

"Ah, General Ragdar," General Panchali said wistfully to his big-nosed opposite number, stroking his silver beard which came to a point halfway down his broad chest. "I feel a deep sadness in my heart on this day." His narrow eyes, set in a face as weatherbeaten as a piece of driftwood, surveyed the immense mountainscape that surrounded them. For the last six months they had pursued the enemy right up into the Himalayas, seeking to wipe them out. The highest peaks in the world poked through the clouds, their tops disappearing above the ken of mortal man. In any direction they could see for over a hundred miles in air that was as clear and cool as a mountain spring. Snow dotted the slopes around them — and higher, glacial ice sheets, a billion tons worth, always threatening to avalanche and bury everything in their path. The realization that the fighting had died down dismayed him. His expression gave this away.

"What sadness can be found on a day like this?" Ragdar, ten years younger and filled to overflowing with a lust for life, asked his elder. "We have just won a war, we are rich, we are generals of a quarter of a million men who are feared throughout Asia, we have all the women, all the wine a man could drink, we are surrounded by the most beautiful terrain on all of God's poisoned earth — and you feel sadness." Ragdar leaned over and slammed a huge hand across Panchali's back, trying to rouse him from his lethargies.

"I mourn because there is not more war," Panchali replied in his deep bass voice. "To fight — to die — what is life for but these?"

"But what of fine food, gems, slaves — love — women?" his younger compatriot asked with a lascivious smile on his face.

"Love is for rabbits," Panchali said. "For me

women are just intermissions between the main masculine acts of war. I am quickly bored. But tell me," Panchali said suddenly, growing animated. "Do you not feel most alive in battle? With all your senses heightened, speeded up so that every image, every sound and scent is imbued with power—power to bring your existence into a super-fine focus—in which men, worlds, civilizations come and go in the flash of an eye, in a second. When a man comes at me with his sword, I feel transcended, lifted from my body. I can see it all in slow motion, sense everything, can see the foam bubbling up from his steed's mouth, see the way the hoof strikes the ground at an odd angle, and how my enemy's face is filled with a thousand conflicting emotions. This—this is my art, my love. The beauty of the fight. Of one man against another. No chance to grow old. When my reflexes go, then my enemy will win. And he should. And I will go into the realm of the gods, of Vishnu, of Brama and Siva where I'm sure we will all continue to fight amidst the clouds."

"Well said," the younger Ragdar laughed, clapping his hands together. "Perhaps you should have been a poet—not a warrior."

"I fear rather than creating images of beauty, I would instead take my pen and begin stabbing at whoever came near." Both men laughed at the image, and looked at each other with the love that brothers have for one another. Although they were not related by blood, they had fought side by side for the last decade. Many times each had been so close to death he could feel it licking down his spine like a wolf's sandpaper tongue. But the other had appeared out of nowhere with swinging sword and blazing 9mm sub-machinegun and the enemy was destroyed. They had worked their way up in the ranks of the Royal Sikh Army—the "Royal" in the name being a vestige of the old imperial days of the British Empire when the Sikhs had been the fiercest of the colonial English fighters—and had gained a worldwide reputation for their ferocity, bravery, and keen military intelligence. The crafty Russians had allowed them to keep the name—for they understood the power of military tradition to motivate men, to make them storm through battlefields carrying their banner high.

The Sikhs were given wealth, power, and masses of weapons and ammunition. In return they took on the enemies of the New World Soviet Empire—those "barbarian tribes" that Moscow felt were the most threatening. They were an age-old breed of man—mercenaries. Not worrying a whole lot about who they were fighting or why—but carrying out their destinies of being warriors—of killing, of routing armies. The gods wished it thus.

"There is truth in what you say," General Ragdar said as he pulled his high-spirited stallion away from the edge of a steep slope that fell out below them thousands upon thousands of feet to the rubbled bottom. "Battle does quicken the heart, speed up all the faculties. Yet I do it more as my vocation. Yes, I love it—but I love other things as well, Panchali. Spreading the legs of young beautiful women, drinking the best brandies and wines, painting pictures of the sea from my mansion near Calcutta. These things all make *me* feel alive."

"Ah, you are much too sensitive, my young Sikh

warrior. I'm amazed you have lasted this long in the business. A career of killing can take a lot out of a man if he thinks about it too long. I prefer to do what I am best at and leave the fate-wheel, the judgments, to the gods."

They came to a plateau and let the stallions rest for a minute while the two generals stood on the edge looking down at the plain below them. The tents of their troops stretched on for miles in even rows of round goatskin dwellings, the corrals for their stallions set every quarter mile or so. The men were walking outside, barely visible specks from the generals' vantage point, spread out around the camps and environs like an army of ants. Only these ants weren't working—but sitting, reading, wrestling, or swimming in the large lake next to which the Sikh army had temporarily bivouacked. And they deserved it, General Ragdar thought as he gazed down on them with a fond love for those who would die for him. They had all fought as hard as a man—even a Sikh—could fight. And now . . . Now the body would slow down, the heart pace drop to a more civilian rate. Even if it rankled Panchali—the rest of the army needed it. No one goes forever living only on the sight of blood.

"I am bored already," Panchali said with a deep sigh, his sapphire-ringed hand resting on the hilt of his sword as if wanting to draw it. "Soldiers should not sit, rest, sleep in the middle of the day. I have lived too long as a fighter, a general—not to feel sickened by the sight of my men without their guns, their swords ready. Ah, perhaps I am already becoming an anachronism, obsolete as the Empire collapses all around us."

"Not obsolete, Panchali," Ragdar said, "just too successful for your own good. We just vanquished one army, took back an entire nation into the arms of Mother Russia. Congratulate yourself, let your own flesh rest for a moment. I have a whole new shipment of young, ripe girls from the southern steppes—they are beautiful, Panchali. With huge brown eyes like a fawn and skin with the texture of the finest Peking silk. There are too many for me—I am not greedy. I will give you four or five—get your mind off all this peace."

"Yes, yes, you are right," General Panchali said, "I'm turning into a fool." Suddenly they both heard the sound of hooves from behind them and turned to see a messenger with red pennant, tearing up the trail, leaving a cloud of dust all the way down the steep side. Within minutes he reached the plateau and raced toward them. The rider pulled his midnight-black mount to a stop and jumped down. He threw himself to the ground, kneeling far over as was the greeting of all lower ranks to either of the two generals.

"Sikh Panchali—an urgent message direct from the premier."

"Yes, yes, rise up man, what is it?" the general asked with a rising hope in his heart.

"Sir, I know it sounds peculiar, but we decoded the message three times and asked for confirmation—and it is accurate."

"Speak, fool," Panchali said, pulling his sword half out of its emerald-encrusted scabbard, "before you have no head from which to speak."

"S-s-sir, Premier Vassily wishes you to take the entire First Royal Sikh Army by transport jet to the U.S.S.A. where you will join forces with the American Freefighters and battle Colonel Killov, who has attacked Red Army bases throughout the country." The messenger gave the message in one long breath and the moment he finished he gasped for air, his lungs heaving.

"W-w-what?" Ragdar said, almost in a whisper. "I can hardly believe it." His women, his weeks of hedonistic saturation all vanished before his eyes. He looked positively mournful.

"Good," Panchali laughed, holding his arms wide to the sky as if thanking the gods. "Good. The wheel of Karma spins again. We fight again, Ragdar, my wishes have come true. I will have to sample your gourmet treats some other day."

"But to fight *alongside* the rebel American Freefighters," Ragdar mumbled. "It is all so strange. I can't . . ." Ragdar, who liked to see the world in simplistic, easily understood terms, was confused and mystified. They were mercenaries, but never had they fought alongside any man — let alone their lifelong enemies.

"As for me, Sikh Ragdar," Panchali said with a look of supreme satisfaction on his dark lined face, "I don't give a damn who we fight — as long as we get the chance once more to sever heads from their infidel bodies."

Chapter Eleven

"We'll have to go around it," Ted Rockson said, pointing at the rim wall of the mile-wide A-bomb crater that loomed ahead, blocking their way north to Fort Minsk like a monument to the gods of nuclear darkness. He pulled the reins of his 'brid slightly to the right and the long straggly line of Freefighters fell in behind him. Since his conversation with Premier Vassily, the Doomsday Warrior had actually begun believing that they had a chance to thwart Killov's coup d'etat. Even the maddening tit-for-tat—Rona and Kim were still riding right behind him as if to make sure he heard their every biting word—didn't irritate Rockson today. For the first time in days he felt in a positively good mood.

"My, you're looking well today, considering . . ." Rona said with a sweet smile to Kim, who rode almost abreast her, a few feet behind.

"And you too," Kim rejoindered, hitting the psychological tennis ball back. "When one realizes that you're in your mid-thirties and still surprisingly attractive. Why, those sun lines or, are they 'crows feet' eyes and lips are hardly noticeable—except perhaps in bright light. It really is amazing."

"And amazing that your diminutive twig of a body hasn't crumpled out here in the real world," Rona suddenly blurted out as Kim's last barb had stung her. She felt that her face was more striking than the more sweet-girl-next-door looks of her rival—but Kim *was* ten years younger than she. And somewhere in the midst of her fears of losing Rockson, Rona thought perhaps he would want a younger woman, less touched by the acid hands of time.

"All right, you two," Rock said, leaning around in his saddle. "We're going around some high slopes here with lots of loose rock and boulders just itching to slide down if the right sound waves hit them. Sound waves like you two clucking on like a couple of mad hens in the barnyard. Okay. I mean, it's a free country and all that—but not when the whole damned mountain might come down on all of us." They both looked at him with burning eyes, angry at him, at each other, at everything, but clamped their lips tight as vises, the skin turning white and stiff in repressed rage.

The team spread out about 30 yards apart in the standard formation for any potential landslide terrain, so the entire team wouldn't be buried. Rock slowed his 'brid to a crawl to see what effect the clapping hoof beats of the expedition might be having on the shale slopes that stretched up a good half mile into the rainy gray afternoon sky. He had seen several avalanches, almost died in one. And it was not an experience he wanted to repeat.

They rode about a hundred feet from the base of the crater, still strewn with shiny green-glass balls—

dirt and stone melted by the bomb blast a century ago. The jewels of the atomic age. Highly radioactive jewels—death to the unwary collector. Whenever Rockson passed one of the many craters that scarred the face of America like pockmarks that wouldn't disappear, he got the same feeling. A sensation of dread, of darkness, so deep it filled the pit of his stomach, his heart, with waves of nausea and doom. For Rockson could feel the souls of those who had died from the blast. Those whose ashes were mixed into the mountain, their molecules forever and inextricably bound with the radioactive molecules of the nuclear mound. If atoms can cry, then the Doomsday Warrior heard their moans, felt their invisible tears waft down the slopes in waves of drifting blue fog.

"Jeez, it's a spooky one," Rona whispered to Rockson from about ten feet behind.

"Yeah, you can feel it," he whispered back, and realized that he was whispering not just to avoid a landslide but because he felt as if the crater was listening—a malevolent ear taking in all that was said about it. "I hate these fucking things," Rockson suddenly spat out. "Once the Reds are kicked out and President Langford takes over—I'm going to lobby hard for the first order of business to be getting rid of these pus-filled wounds. Our country will never heal, never grow fully green again as long as they exist. It would help lower the rad-level anyway, to fill them in."

"Amen," Rona said as she looked up at the dark slopes alive with a thousand radioactive shadows. The whole damned thing seemed haunted, filled with ghosts, bursting with lost souls glued forever to this one spot. The entire team unconsciously moved a little closer together as shivers rippled along their backbones.

They were but halfway around the manmade obstruction when there was a very low but distinct rumbling sound that seemed to come from far off. Rock raised his hand and the team came to a halt, silent, as they listened intently through the first whistling teeth of the evening wind. It was a deep sound, so low that it was almost inaudible. But its vibration seemed to be traveling through the ground beneath their feet. The 'brids grew nervous and began stomping around. Rockson jumped down from old Snorter and put his ear to the soil. His face drained of color. Mutant psi-instinct sent shivers up his spine.

"I don't exactly know what it is—but something bad is about to happen." He leaped up and onto his 'brid in a single motion and kicked the animal hard on the side.

"Let's get the hell out of here," Rock yelled at the top of his lungs. Snorter took off like something launched from a cannon with the rest of the mutant steeds right behind. But they'd only gone fifty feet or so when the earth began shaking harder—very slowly but rising in intensity every second. The 'brids were able to keep their balance but for how long, Rockson wondered, sure that a full-scale earthquake was about to hit. He waited for the cracks to begin opening in the flesh of the planet; for the men, the animals around him to disappear, screaming their way thousands of feet down into a consuming darkness. Not again—not now, he demanded to unknown gods as he leaned forward on Snorter's back, slapping its shoulder to make the 'brid move faster. But the team needed no more motivation than they were already getting and flew along, their feet barely touching the ash and gravel ground.

Suddenly the ground beneath them seemed to convulse several times as if the earth itself was about to vomit and an explosion of rock and red lava shot a thousand feet into the air from the crater next to them.

"Jesus Christ," Rock blurted out as Snorter slowed to about half speed, trying to keep its balance in the midst of the upheaval. For a split second Rockson thought it was an A-bomb, as a mass of dark gas lifted into a mushroom-cloud shape high in the sky. But in another second, he realized what it was—a volcanic eruption. The dormant A-bomb crater had stirred something up that took a hundred years to get to the surface—but it had arrived with trumpets blaring.

The earth settled slightly but the huge crater continued to shoot up a torrent of fiery dust and glowing rocks. Clouds of spewing gas and particles settled over the Freefighters, blotting out the sky, making it as dark as a moonless night.

Rock slowed the terrified 'brid even more, pulling at the reins with all his might to make the creature obey his commands. Turning in his saddle, he yelled out, "Throw your rope to the man in front of you. We've got to tie the 'brids together or we're goners." Rona passed the word back and as they continued slowly forward through the blizzard of black, ropes were tossed and anchored around the saddlehorns. Safely tethered, Rockson built up speed, literally

149

pulling the rest behind. The blind leading the blind — they'd have to get out fast. The gases of volcanos, Rockson knew, were often poisonous. A few minutes of breathing the foul-smelling stuff that was passing for air and they might be dead. And if the gas didn't get them, he could see a half mile behind, even through the thick curtains of falling hot ash, glowing rivers of lava bubbling over the lip of the crater and down, like a cup that runneth over.

Rockson struggled to keep his eyes focused. The air was already becoming so thick with soot and noxious fumes that it filled his lungs with a racking pain. Tremors nearly threw the mounts off their stride.

"Use your neckerchiefs," Rock screamed again, barely able to be heard even by Rona, who was right behind him. He took his own sweat collector from around his neck and reached around, fumbling for his water gourd. Rock ripped the top from it and poured the contents over the handkerchief, completely drenching it. He wrapped the makeshift gas mask around his face and within seconds felt more clear-headed as he was able to suck in relatively breathable air. The nostrils of the 'brids had closed, using an evolutionary adaptation of small chambers in their nasal cavities to filter out particles. But even the multi-talented mutant mount-mammals couldn't filter out the gas.

Somehow, though, the 'brids kept going, heaving with great rasping breaths but not slackening their paces one step. The ground seemed to slow to a low rumble and behind them they could hear the volcano roaring out her evacuation of the earth's burning stomach. The spout of red and white-hot glowing material spewed forth shooting off for miles in every direction. The main river of red lava rose higher and higher over the mouth of the nuke crater, spilling its deadly contents onto the earth's sandy flesh as if pouring from a broken spigot.

Rockson kept on in the direction he had been heading when the atomic hell-hole blew its heap — straight toward the desert. They could circle back toward Fort Minsk, their objective, later. The main thing on the agenda was survival. But as the air grew thicker and thicker with dust and sickening smells, it didn't look like a good bet. He turned and could just make out Rona and her tethered 'brid following quickly behind him. Her head was wobbling from side to side, but as her eyes caught his she gave a feeble nod to show she was conscious. Rockson motioned for her to check Kim and slowly, as if half asleep, the red-haired Freefighter twisted around in her saddle to check her love-adversary. Rock swung forward again and tried to see through the cocoon of volcanic debris that completely encased them now, in search of any trees or cacti or gulleys. They were traveling almost blind, slowly, and he felt as if he was going through a tunnel with no lights. But Rockson knew that the 'brids had a sixth sense for obstacles; he'd seen them perform in blindfolded tests conducted by Shecter's bio-unit. All he could do was hold on tight. He wished to hell the women were not along on this mission.

They'd gone about a mile and a half when the ash fog grew less dense. The prairie came into view, stretching off flat and featureless, bathed with the diffuse glow of the obscured sun and the fire of the orange mouth of the volcano, which vomited its load like a bad supper.

Rockson looked around, at last able to see the full team, still roped together, stretching back fifty yards. Everyone was still hanging on, though some of them looked ready for embalming, draped over their 'brids' shoulders face-forward like they were out cold. But it was what was coming up behind them that caught Rockson's horrified eye. A tidal wave of lava, sweeping forward, setting ablaze every tree, every cactus, every scurrying plains creature that it encountered. A wall of searing mud and molten rock five feet high, burning across the landscape from every side of the crater, its molten stone glowing like some immense beacon a thousand feet high, a light that could have been seen from the moon. And it was coming straight toward them at a fast clip, faster than they were moving, bubbles and hellish foam licking along the tops of the red waves.

"Faster, dammit, faster," Rock screamed in Snorter's ear, kicking him as hard as he had ever kicked the creature in their long relationship. The beast seemed to understand Rockson's super intensity, that death was imminent. Snorter started to gallop, its big furry head lifting high into the air and down again like a piston running the animal machine beneath it. The rest of the team somehow jerked along and kept pace, their heads pulled forward by the nylon rope of the 'brid ahead. They had no choice—either they slammed their legs down again and again to the point of collapse or they fell and died. And if just one fell now—all would perish.

The volcanic lava wall pushed closer, seeming to

accelerate as it neared them. Though still a half-mile off, Rockson could feel the crackling heat of the molten granite on his back. They would be mere puffs of smoke if that stuff caught up with them—swallowed without a burp. He scanned forward, searching desperately for anything—he didn't know what—when he saw a thin blue line off to the right. It was hard to tell if it was a mirage from all the crap in the air or not—but as they drew closer, the blue grew richer and wider and the lapping waves became real water, as a river came into view. The Freefighters beelined for the tributary as the volcano shook with H-bomb force once again and unleashed another explosion, larger than the first, that reached up into the clouds and swallowed them whole in its black ash jaws. The damned thing was going to take out this whole section of the country, Rock thought as they rode hell-bent for leather toward the river ahead. Wouldn't even be bad. He had seen the ash of volcanos in other parts of the country act as fertilizer, creating a rich topsoil after a few years where plants grew in wild profusion, freeing the earth from radioactive poisons of the surface. Only Rock didn't want to be fertilizer—no matter how much it enriched the ecosystem.

They reached the bank of the river, which was a hundred feet wide at this juncture and raging like a wildcat with rapids creating a billowing foam of whitecaps. But there was no time to go looking for a nice comfy spot to cross—not with a grinding wall of incendiary mud coming at them with the speed of a racehorse.

"Archer!" Rockson screamed out, restraining his

anxious 'brid, who wanted to jump into the river to escape the heat that it too could feel on its hindquarters. "Archer!" the Doomsday Warrior screamed again. The bear-sized mountain man cut his rope loose, came flying out of the middle of the pack atop his own monstrous steed — even larger than Rockson's, with legs like pillars — which it needed to carry the 380 pounds-plus that rode it.

"R-R-Rooocksson," the huge near-mute croaked out like a frog in heat.

"Archer," Rockson said, pointing across the rough waters. "That wide oak tree on the other side. See it? Shoot one of your cable-arrows into it. Do you understand me?"

"Arrrchher shoooot treee," the giant groaned back as he swung his huge steel-wired crossbow around to the front. He reached around behind him and took a narrow but deep spool from one of his saddle bags and attached the quarter-inch alloy cable to the back end of the arrow, resting it in the firing slot. Putting one leg up on the 'brid's neck, Archer positioned the front of the yard-wide crossbow on his knee and sighted up. His target was a gnarled age-old tree, six feet wide at the base, which drooped wide leafy branches out over the opposite edge of the river, creating shadows where fish swam to hide from their bigger-jawed relatives.

The mountain man let his body settle, waiting several seconds until his arm stopped shaking from the adrenaline rush. Then he gently squeezed the wide trigger, which was big enough for a finger as large as most men's wrists. The arrow shot from the front end of the primitive but powerful weapon with the slightest whoosh as it sliced the air with a razor head. It flew unerringly just above the river, which reached up as if trying to suck it down, and slammed into the oak a yard above the ground. The arrow hit with tremendous velocity and the specially designed arrow sank in eight inches, burying itself forever in the dense wood fiber.

"Give it to me," Rockson yelled above the din of the volcanic maelstrom unfolding all around them and the frantic braying of the now completely unhinged hybrid horses. He jumped down from his 'brid and grabbed the spool of cable from Archer's hands, running over to a large tree by the shore. Rock wrapped the thin steel mesh cable, tested at up to a ton for tensile strength, around the wide trunk and leaped back up on Snorter and started the 'brid forward before he hit the saddle.

"I'll go first," he yelled at the disoriented squad of Freefighters, who were dizzy from the gases and coated from head to foot in a fine layer of ink-black soot. "Take your link-up ropes from your saddlebags—every one of you has one," the Doomsday Warrior cried out as he held one of them up, his eyes glued to the throbbing wall of white-hot slag coming toward them in a rushing waterfall of flame. "Slip the lower clamp around the saddle ring and when you get your 'brid into the water—fit the other clamp around the wire. Don't screw up—or you're dead." He prayed that his words had stirred them from their near comatose states—there would be no second chances.

Rockson headed his 'brid into the ripping river at full gallop, creating a big splash. But the animal was a sure swimmer and headed in the direction Rockson pulled the reins. He slipped the hinge clasp over the cable and breathed a sigh of relief. At least they wouldn't get swept off. Snorter swam forward, guided by the constant tug of the cable, as Rockson spun around on his saddle so he was facing the other way. The rest of the team steered their mounts into the river one after another, hitting the blue with splashes of white and then linking up. They all seemed to be doing it right and the cold water rushing over them woke them up with frigid slaps.

As Snorter swam toward the center of the river it grew rougher, the whitecaps bigger, hitting hard. They slammed into the 'brid's side, trying to sweep it downriver. The huge animal slowed to a crawl as it fought furiously beneath the surface with all four legs, paddling the wide oars at a fast pace. The whole lower portion of the mammal's body was pulled sideways by the current, forcing it to swim at a nearly 45-degree angle. But swim it did, never faltering, never doubting it could make it. The massive mountain of fire was moving right up to the other bank, snapping a grove of trees two hundred yards off and chewing them down like flies, sending up little fogs of super-heated sap that were ignited by the heat before they rose fifty feet. Animals trapped by the killing lava rushed forward in streaks of furry lightning and dove head-first into the waters without a second thought and began paddling, holding their heads high up above the lapping liquid. Beavers, gray foxes, desert armadillos—all swam feet apart as if in an animal olympics—to see who would live.

At last the 'brid touched solid ground and hoisted itself up out of the water, hitting the shore at full stride. Rock leapt down, reaching the ground before the animal could stop, and ran to the sandy shore yelling encouragement to the others.

"Keep going—you're almost here," he yelled out to Rona, cupping his hands like a megaphone. He could see that she was barely hanging on and was being buffeted around in the saddle like a pingpong ball. But she had wrapped her arms around the hybrid's neck and was clutching the thick furred mane tightly with both fists.

Rockson's attention was suddenly diverted to the back of the watery stampede of men and animals as the screeching neighs of an animal in mortal terror filled the air. Somehow one of the clasps had come loose from the cable—and man and animal were instantly swept beneath the wire and down the river. Rockson opened his eyes wide to see who it was— Karston—one of the siege-experts Rock had picked for the mission. The speed of the river picked up enormously just a few hundred feet downriver and waves rose up to six and seven feet from the surface, slamming wildly around in grinding jaws of white. Karston, tied to his mount, hit the roughest part of the foam and disappeared beneath the waves, the hybrid's legs spinning over several times before vanishing into the lower reaches.

Knowing the man was dead, Rockson turned his gaze back to the living. The rest of the party was struggling but somehow forging their way across, and within sixty seconds most of them were up on the far shore, some laughing and nearly hysterical that they had survived sure death. McCaughlin brought up the rear and Rock kept an anxious eye on the man as his mount moved at a turtle's pace, its nostrils and eyes only inches above the stinging waves. The big Scotsman hung on tenaciously, his legs wrapped tighter than an anemone around a clam to his 'brid's back. And behind him, tethered by twin ropes, were the three 'brids the supply man was trailing, all of them churning up the waters in their own desperate reach for survival.

The river of fire met the river of water behind them and the sky filled with smoke and steam from the concussive rendezvous. The vaporized liquid shot out like superheated water from a broken pipe, streaming out across the river. Rockson reached out to guide McCaughlin's 'brid, who found it hard footing, but somehow between them they pulled the last member of the team up onto dry land.

Rock mounted his 'brid again and headed the team away from the river. The million-gallon flow of water had stopped the lava—for now. Who knew how much it could swallow up—or how much the volcano was going to pump out as it continued to belch forth like a giant factory chimney on a 24-hour work shift.

They rode for a good ten minutes until Rock knew they were miles off and safe—until the next thing that tried to do them in, anyway. The team halted and turned their 'brids around, the fighters saying not a word. The volcano was eerily beautiful from a distance—they could appreciate it now that they knew it wouldn't burn them alive. It spouted up a geyser of fire in a perfectly shaped plume that had stabilized at a height of about 800 feet. It erupted with a fiery grace, its sheets of flame forming a flower-like shape before cresting and falling back down in wide symmetrical curves onto the sea of red rock below, where it joined in the wild push of the inanimate matter like lemmings on the path of least resistance.

The gases of the volcano had collected high in the atmosphere and were creating hypnotic rainbow effects, as if a sheen of oil had been sprayed across the heavens. Luminescent purples, blues, greens, and golds shimmered and meshed with one another in an almost living undulation of color and shape. All along the river a line of steam rose up, creating a hot wet fog that covered the vegetation for miles, not killing most of it, but wilting it, drooping leaves and flowers so they looked as if they were drunk, and in their intoxication had fallen flat.

Chapter Twelve

The gases of the volcano formed an immense brown hemisphere of soot that covered the land for twenty miles around the spouting center. Twelve hours later Rockson and his party could still see the fountain of burning rock gushing into the sky as if trying to reach the beckoning fires of the sun ninety million miles away. Rock had decided to make a wide circle around the perimeter of the gas. Everyone on the team had already breathed too much of the stuff — and they were all looking a little green around the gills. It would add a day to their journey to Fort Minsk, but they were ahead of schedule by nearly two days and could afford the delay.

So they headed east for half a day and then north again. The land grew thick with vegetation, small ponds, and animals — unicorn deer, poison-quilled porcupines, flying squirrels with feathered wings — all moved in nature's harmony around the weary fighters. Toward night they bagged a big buck and roasted it over a spitfire, cutting off huge chunks and wolfing them down like savages. Rock had okayed the feast. The men needed a rest — some good food — and the nurturing warmth of a fire. They were smack in the middle of nowhere—between prairie and the next mountain range—with no Red forts for a hundred miles. It would be safe. It would have to be. One couldn't go on endlessly without some sort of respite, some relief.

They slept under the trillion-starred sky, Rona and Kim continuing to lie on each side of Rockson, but far enough away so it didn't appear that either of them was on the make for him. It was just accidental that their sleeping sacks ended up there. A biting wind from the north made them all burrow deep into their synth/down bags—but it also cleared away much of the sulphur and other gases that the earth had regurgitated.

By morning, after a night of breathing the clear frosty air, everyone—even the 'brids—was alert, bright-eyed, their lungs cleaned out. The attack team broke camp and headed out. Rona and Kim, since they were feeling their oats, went at it almost instantly once they hit the trail.

"Darling, had the most frightful dream about you last night," Kim said, turning her small blond head toward Rona, whose 'brid trotted happily along a yard away, ears up.

"Oh really? How fascinating," Rona said, tossing her flaming red hair back around one side of her head as if it really wasn't particularly intriguing at all—but quite boring.

"Yes, you turned into a giant spider and were waving all these hairy legs at everyone."

"Hairy legs—I would think that would be more in your department," Rona said with a stifled yawn, referring to the fact that her rival didn't shave her legs, although her downy blond covering was hardly noticeable. Rona, on the other hand, always the female, brought razors along even on military expeditions, stripping the fast-growing dark hairs on her own calves every few days. "Didn't try to *eat* you, did I?" Rona laughed with a cold quick giggle. "Spiders *do* eat little *weak* fruitflies."

"Oh, you tried," Kim smiled, "so I had to shoot you. I felt terrible about it, apologized to everyone. But there it was—you had turned into a giant, ugly spider—it wasn't my fault."

"Oh, little one," Rona said icily, "in a million years, if every second of them was your lucky day, you couldn't take me with a howitzer in each hand. I'd split your sweet head open with one chop. Of course, only in a dream."

"But darling, I left my howitzers at home," Kim answered immediately. "Prefer to use one of my bear stoppers here." She glanced down at her shining .45's sitting on each hip, waiting for the next battle that would bring them to life.

"Come on, you two," Rockson said, leaning around in the saddle and looking sternly at the two women he loved. "No one in my outfit talks about doing someone else in—no matter how much they're playing around. Okay? Keep your barbs friendly."

"Of course, Rock," Kim said, looking genuinely abashed. She didn't want to appear bloodthirsty in her lover's eyes.

"I'm sorry," Rona smiled in her most come-hither look at the Doomsday Warrior, who broke into a broad smile. He still had no better way of dealing

163

with either or both of them but to grin idiotically and say nothing. He crossed his fingers. Somehow the thing *would* work itself out. Thank god they had a war to fight.

Both were back at it again within minutes, unable to resist the nasty temptation like a moth flying closer and closer to the flame, playing with itself, testing its wings to see what it will take to stroke them into fire.

"Little one," Rona began this time, a syrupy tone in her voice. "No one on the team has the nerve to say it — but when are you going to wash those fatigues? They're starting to — well — smell rather strong."

"Wash them — oh yes, I had planned to back at the river, but a volcano so rudely interrupted me," Kim said in a frost-coated tone. She cast a wicked glance at her rival, this time stung by one of Rona's many attempts to icepick her way through Kim's defenses. It was somehow ironic that the very characteristics each possessed were what they attacked in the other. Rona, who was always going after Kim's small stature and girlish qualities, was herself intensely female and played it to the hilt. She prided herself on her body and dressed in skintight clothing, both to be appreciated and to permit quick movement of all her limbs, since she was highly skilled in a number of martial arts. Kim, on the other hand, who needled Rona for her largeness and masculine strength, clothed herself in half-torn combat fatigues and an olive-green field jacket with pockets stuffed full of ammo and food. To disguise her own small size and lack of male strength, she dressed the part of a jockey-sized combat vet, disheveled, unbathed — and if she'd had whiskers, unshaven. It made her feel tougher, a little more able to cope with the unrelenting pressure of being in a man's world of death and blood.

"I guess your clothes keep fresher longer," Kim said, looking over at the form-fitting spandex combat bodysuit that her rival was wearing. "But then, there's a need to emphasize the body parts that prove your masculine body is really female, so it's no wonder. I think you need a few repairs, though—you're busting at the seams in a few places there. Guess they couldn't take the strain of that buffalo bottom and those elephant thighs."

"Listen, you grape-chested little twit," Rona hissed back through compressed lips, restraining herself with every ounce of her will from lashing out with a punch. It would be easy, she thought, just one lousy punch. But then whoever struck the other first would lose points with Rock.

"Hold it," Rockson said suddenly, his voice cutting through the air with the commanding tone of a bullet. "Hear something." He held up his hand, signaling a stop, and the rest of the team fell in behind them, patting their restless 'brids to keep quiet. They had entered a long lush valley with treed slopes rising several hundred feet on each side. Rockson thought he heard the clatter of a bunch of animals nearby. He looked sharply around the hillsides covered with little islands of thorned bush and up to the treeline along the top ridges. It would be the perfect place for an ambush—the thought went through his mind with an intensity that made him think his sixth sense was picking up on something.

"Battle status," the Doomsday Warrior said out of the side of his mouth to the rest of the fighters, who had come to a half circle behind him. They unhitched their holsters, and .45's and Liberator rifles came swinging around as nervous eyes searched for an unseen enemy.

"There, ahead," Rona yelled out. Rockson pulled hard on Snorter's reins and the big 'brid spun around as if on a dime. Rock stared down the center of the valley, in the direction they had been heading. He had to resist the urge to rub his eyes. For standing in their way, mounted on twenty palomino hybrids, was a war party of American Indians. They sat impassively, frozen like statues atop their equally motionless steeds. Their faces and arms were covered with stripes and designs, slashes of red and blue and green that crisscrossed over their bodies, giving them a fierce and demonic appearance. On their heads sat feathered headdresses with rows of multicolored feathers from at least a dozen different species, falling over their broad copper shoulders and down their backs.

"Indians," Detroit said, his eyes bulging out of his sweat-covered black face. "I can't believe it. No one's seen 'em since the war. They were thought to be extinct, except for the *Crazy Alligator* tribe.*

"These look like the real thing," Rockson said, his sixth sense buzzing away like a broken alarm in the center of his skull.

He remembered the fires he had seen up on ledges in his travels, the smoke signals rising into the sky in puffs of communication between mountain ranges. He had always known someone was out there besides trappers and mountain-men.

*See Doomsday Warrior #2.

166

"They, uh, don't look too friendly," Rona said, nervously fingering the trigger on her Liberator. "I think that stuff on their faces isn't just for cosmetic beauty."

"No—it's war paint, definitely war paint," Rock said. "And something tells me we've been picked to be the guys on the receiving end. But hold your fire. Maybe they'll let us pass—"

The Indians suddenly unfroze and lifted rifles to their shoulders, sending down a fusillade of slugs toward the halted resistance fighters, who slid down against the back of their 'brids in a flash and then sat up again, returning the volley. The sheer firepower of the Freefighting forces sent the Indians on the run as they ripped their 'brids around and hightailed it along the valley floor.

"Freefighters attack!" Rockson yelled as Snorter shot forward, head down, nostrils flaring. The force took up pursuit of the whooping Indians who rode bareback, facing around toward their pursuers, firing with both arms. One of them stood up on the back of his galloping 'brid and sighted up Rockson. But the Doomsday Warrior had also spent years firing from atop a running animal and made his arms rock-steady, his shoulders rising and falling like shock absorbers from the pounding hooves of the 'brid. Rock pulled the trigger at the same instant the standing Indian did and their slugs passed within inches of each other, cutting whistling trajectories toward their targets. The Indian's slug caught Rock's 'brid just along the shoulder, but the thick-hided animal barely felt it as the bullet only dug in about a half an inch, exiting again immediately. Snorter didn't even notice it. Rock's 9mm bullet found a home for good, in the Indian's nose, disintegrating it on contact into a bloody spray, before heading into the brain where it ground up everything it touched.

The Freefighters' ears were suddenly inundated with the sound of a thousand war cries as the ridges on each side of the valley were filled with horse-mounted warriors holding rifles high in their arms. They stretched in long lines on both sides, two hundred feet above Rockson, who took in the scene with cold eyes, realizing they had been tricked. He remembered a film about General Custer, starring Errol Flynn, that he'd seen back in Century City. The cavalryman had been suckered in exactly this way and then surrounded by thousands of braves. And he and his men had been massacred.

One of the younger chiefs, identifiable by his immense feather bonnet rode down, holding a war staff high in the air. He came down the slope at a slow even pace, not batting an eyelash as if he didn't care whether the men below fired at him or not, whether he lived or died. Several of the Freefighters sighted through their scopes, but Rockson barked out a quick "No!" and they lowered them again. With what must have been at least a thousand of the painted braves on every side of them, Rockson didn't feel like throwing their lives away. Maybe a quick tongue could save them.

The Indian, with his own distinctive cosmetic col-oration—yellow, green, and white stripes running parallel from temple to chin—rode right up to the Doomsday Warrior, stopped, and spat down at the ground near Snorter's foreleg.

"Friendly guy," Detroit muttered, clenching a grenade tightly in his right hand, ready for release at Rockson's command.

"Ease up, everybody," the Doomsday Warrior said, gritting his teeth. "Don't make a move, act relaxed. And smile." Rockson remembered the lectures of the now-deceased Professor Perkins and the anthropology people back at Century City. How, when one first encountered strange races, even those of the most savage-seeming nature, the first thing to do was act friendly — and smile. So all the Freefighers put on huge, false, lip-stretching grins and stared at the poker-faced Indian.

The chief, or whatever he was, began sending out a torrent of angry words at them, sneering and spitting again every few seconds for punctuation. Rock called up Nielson, whom he had chosen for his knowledge of languages and communication skills as well as for his fighting talents.

"See if you can figure out what the hell he's jabbering about," Rock said to the intense ruddy-cheeked linguist.

"Sure Rock, I'll give it a try — but I ain't promising." Nielson began making a variety of sign-language signals with his hands — a language the anthro boys swore was an exact rendering of the 1800s Indian sign-language. The Indian looked on in scorn at first, but then, recognizing a sign here and there, responded with various fists, arm arrangements, and finger patterns. Within a minute the two men were exchanging rapid sequences of silent signals. To Rockson, the gestures seemed a lot like the ancient

169

Buddhist *mudras* he had studied.

At last the Indian stopped and let his arms fall to his sides, once again looking at Rockson with utmost contempt, as if he were a bug that should be squashed. Nielson turned to the Doomsday Warrior, a solemn look on his usually jovial face.

"Rock," Nielson said, looking down at the ground as if he didn't want to be the messenger bearing the bad news. "The situation is, more or less, either we surrender to them—they're Sioux—immediately and throw down our weapons—or they'll slaughter us to a man. I tried all kinds of things on them, even bribery—but these guys got their minds made up. I mean—look around you."

Rockson didn't have to. He had seen war parties from other kinds of tribes, other societies. They didn't go home empty-handed. He quickly juggled the odds in his head. He and his men had some heavy artillery—their Liberators, grenades, McCaughlin's .50 Cal packed away on one side of a supply 'brid, but instantly usable. Yet . . . He surveyed both hills again, not even able to see the end of either line of screaming braves, some of them shooting off wildly into the sky, impatient to begin the attack. There was no way in hell he and his men would come out victorious. It would be another Custer's Last Stand, another massacre. He sighed, remembering a book he had read about esoteric Comanche torture skills. But what could they do?

"We're surrendering, folks," Rock said softly, looking around at his people, the lives he was responsible for.

"Rock, no!" Detroit and Chen exclaimed simultaneously as Archer looked on, fiddling with his cross-bow that was loaded with an explosive arrow, ready to be launched into the Indian ranks. A thousand-to-fifteen odds were okay with Archer.

"Yes," Rock said firmly and louder this time. "Keep any hidden weapons you have on you. But drop the Liberators and pistols. It's certain death to shoot it out here. We don't have to prove our hero-ics — there'll be a second chance, I promise you." The men were loathe to give themselves up to the war-striped braves who surrounded them. God knew what their fate would be — better to die in a pool of hot blood right here than be tortured, mutilated. But Rockson was their leader — and though it turned their guts to do it — the Freefighters unstrapped their weap-ons and let them fall around them to the weed-covered ground.

The chief who had been conducting the sign lan-guage held the war staff to the sky and waved it slowly back and forth. Its streamers, made of blue feathers, swung in the wind like wings trying to fill with air. The braves on the valley slopes screeched out victory cries and fired their rifles in unison. They descended, a blanket of thousands, covering the valley slopes, and completely surrounded Rockson and his party until they were lost inside a circle of painted faces and impenetrable brown eyes looking at them like the merciless dead stare of the moon.

The younger warriors jumped down from their mounts and collected the discarded arms. They held the powerful Liberators up in the air, looking at the clips and the streamlined features with fascination. They had apparently never seen that kind of weapon before—most of their own rifles were old hunting models—Winchesters and Brownings left over from the long-ago war. Then they proceeded to bind the Freefighters roughly with leather thongs, which the Indians tied behind their backs, and lead them away atop their 'brids. Now that they had taken the enemy prisoner, the Indians seemed to relax a little, laughing and joking with one another over their easy score. Rock prayed that he hadn't made a mistake—that they wouldn't just be butchered immediately—or worse. He saw many a brave eyeing Rona and Kim.

Chapter Thirteen

Buffalo-hide teepees stretched off in long uneven rows like pine cones fallen from winter branches as Rockson and the Freefighting expedition were led into the Sioux village. Squaws carrying babies suckling at their breasts came out to greet the returning heroes and jeer at their captives. The smaller boys shot mock arrows from unstrung bows, practicing for their later roles as hunters and fighters. The Freedomfighters were paraded through the entire camp in and around just about every cone-shaped, hairy-hided tent in the damned place.

"Probably don't get too many prisoners around here," Detroit whispered through his teeth to Chen, who rode behind him, trying to work his hands free of his bonds. "So they want to get every bit of mileage out of it they can."

"Just pretend you're a hero being welcomed home rather than a prisoner about to be acupunctured with arrows — and you'll feel fine," the Chinese Freefighter said to Detroit without turning his head.

"Yeah, feel better already," Detroit groaned. He just didn't feel like dying today. At last the Indians grew tired of the public display and the prisoners were taken to the central square filled with large bonfires which were kept burning all the time. A constant stream of young buckskinned squaws kept coming out of the surrounding woods carrying armloads of dead wood and branches to feed the flames. Medicine men danced around the fires wearing whole buffalo heads—horns, fake eyeballs, swollen white tongues and all, the thick brown fur necks falling almost to their stomachs. They yelled out the deep magical incantations of their ancestors' spirits and called on the buffalo gods to grant their wishes. Skinny dogs ran barking around the Freefighters' legs as they were taken down from their 'brids and led to a long horizontal hitching pole where their bound hands were promptly tied behind their backs along the thirty-foot length.

The victorious braves dismounted and gathered in front of them, some of their feather headdresses hanging down nearly to their ankles. Hunting knives dangled from their rawhide belts and intricately ornamented rifles from their shoulders. They seemed to delight in intimidating their captives and stared at them, laughing, turning to one another with cool self-congratulations. They pointed to the two women who were tied side by side and laughed louder and more coarsely, as scores of lips were licked in anticipation.

The young chief who had demanded their surrender back in the valley walked over to Nielson, untied him, and began communicating with the hand signs again.

"He wants to know who we are," Nielson said to Rockson who stood tied, two men down from him.

"He's Shom-ga-na."

"Tell him everything—tell him the truth," Rock said. "Our only chance is to get these fellows on our side. Tell him we're Americans like him and his people and our only enemy is the Reds. Shit! Tell him we're happy to make his acquaintance!"

Nielson gasped in horror, trying to figure out how to communicate such metaphysical concepts as "enemy" and "truth," but began frantically wiggling away with both hands as the rest of the tribe looked on mystified by the captive's motions.

"He says he and his people—*they* are the real Americans. That the white man came and stole his land and nearly destroyed it. Now his people, the New Sioux Nation, will take it all back again."

"Tell him he's right," Rockson yelled over. "Tell him every fucking word he's saying is true. That our ancestors made many mistakes and committed injustices. But now we face a threat that will destroy us all—even the gods in the clouds."

Again Nielson did his hand tricks and after much asking of questions back and forth with fingers, the Freefighter linguistics expert again spoke out to Rockson, his voice becoming more alarmed with every exchange.

"He says not only did we screw up the whole world—but that our coming across the sacred plains angered the Volcano God and it erupted because of us. And Rock," Nielson gulped audibly, "he says they have to sacrifice us to the God-of-Fire now to set things right again."

"Great," Rockson said, spitting out a gob of disgusted foam into the hard-packed black soil. "Out of the volcano—into the frying pan."

One of the older chiefs, whose face was like a prune filled with a thousand lines carved into the dark red skin, yelled out impatiently from a deerskin throne a hundred feet away. Ten other top Indian war chiefs sat on slightly lower chairs on each side of him and waited, stone-faced, for the proceedings to begin. Three gigantic braves with muscles rippling like steel cables along their arms came and untied the captive on the right side of the pole. It was Thalsberg, one of the youngest men Rock had chosen for the trip due to his sharp-shooting ability and his knowledge of Russian fortification architecture. The man tried to kick out at the painted braves but they took a few blows and grabbed his legs, trussing him up with tight rawhide bindings carrying him away from the pole and over to the largest bonfire which burned dead center in the cleared square, fed a constant flow of fuel from a human conveyor belt of squaws that stretched off to the woods a hundred yards away.

Thalsberg writhed in the Indians' grasp like a creature possessed, twisting his hips, whipping his head around trying to smash them. But all was to no avail. The braves walked with their human package right up to the edge of the roaring fire, twenty feet in diameter, flames rising high into the darkening sky as evening fell. Rock yelled to Nielson, who made signs for 'no.'

The Indians pulled their glistening, sweat-coated arms all the way back and with a heave, threw the struggling Freefighter 10 feet into the flames. He crashed down onto the burning timbers and coals and screamed out so loud that some of the skinny dogs that were watching it all yelped in fear and darted off sideways.

The coals and flames ripped into Thalsberg's body like ravenous teeth and set the skin aboil. From their vantage point, every one of the prisoners could clearly see the flesh turn red at first, then brown, then black as it burst into an oily flame. And the man's face—the lips pulled back so far that the gums and all the teeth were visible as the mouth stretched open wide enough to emit the ear-shattering screams that came out. But not for long. Fire, though the most painful way of dying, kills one relatively quickly. Within fifteen seconds the screams stopped and the body in the cool forgetfulness of trauma shock, ceased its mad jerkings. All the flesh was quickly consumed by the intense heat of the roaring human oven and the bones poked through, the marrow bubbling out the ends and dropping in sizzling pops onto the logs below.

Rock's eyes were moist as he realized that he had made the wrong choice—that they were all going to die like that—and *he* was responsible. It was one of the very few times in his life that the Doomsday Warrior wished he was dead so he wouldn't have to see what was going to happen next.

One of the junior chiefs, a one-eyed badly scarred man standing at the front ranks of the crowds grouped around the square moved forward suddenly toward the prisoners. He headed right for Kim and looked down at her with bestial lust. Then he reached forward and, pulling her field jacket open, ripped her sweatshirt off her body. She stood there, trying to be brave as the cruel face, half its teeth missing, took in the naked breasts standing out proudly in the cool night air. The Indian reached both hands forward and clamped them over the soft globes of flesh, squeezing them so hard that Kim cried out in pain.

Rona, tied next to her, had no love lost for her rival, but if anyone was going to bash her little head in it would be a Wallender, not a foul-breathed, scar-faced Indian. She pulled back her right leg as far as it would go and swung it forward, putting her hips and all her body into the motion. The long leg and booted foot flew out like a striking rattler in a blur of black and caught the brave just beneath the ribs. He wheezed out hard and then crumpled up in a heap on the ground, gasping for air. The nearby Indians couldn't believe their eyes at first — that a mere woman could unleash a blow that took Cha-wamga, one of their toughest men nearly out. But the incredulity turned to rage within seconds and they started forward on Cha-wamga's command, reaching for their long blades, ready to take care of them all right here and now.

"Tell them I challenge their gods," Rock screamed over to Nielson, who was looking on in horror, debating whether to take on the advancing ranks as only his hands were free.

"Tell him I demand the right of a warrior to take the test of the gods — you hear me?" Rock screamed. Not knowing what the hell Rockson was talking about, Nielson frantically tried to get the idea across to the Indian he had been signalling with, who stood, arms folded impassively across his painted chest, two yards in front of him. Shom-ga-na looked at Nielson's hands almost in spite of himself, and as the

178

message penetrated his mind he let out a yell, ran in front of the pole-tied prisoners, and held up his arms, stopping the braves with knives in their hands and blood in their eyes from going a step further. He turned toward the great Chief Bright Sun, the man who had brought the tribe back to the old ways, the good ways, and yelled out a stream of words. The chief's face grew even tighter, his lips settling into a very displeased look as the sub-chiefs on each side muttered angrily, slamming their fists onto the armrests of their buffalo-skin mini-thrones. The crowd whispered to one another, suddenly subdued and angry.

The Sioux communicator turned back toward Nielson and sent out patterns of signs with quick stiff fingers.

"Rock, I don't know what the hell your demand means or why it worked—but he told me they're not going to kill us now and that the initiator of the challenge should come forward—to meet his maker."

"Good work!" Rock said. It was the chance he had been waiting for—an out, an opportunity to pit his skills against theirs. The sign-language Indian walked forward and cut Rockson and Nielson free from the pole, taking the wrist thong in his hands and pulling the Doomsday Warrior forward. He motioned for Nielson to follow and the three of them walked through the buzzing, threatening masses of braves until they reached Chief Bright Sun and his ten-man ruling council, where they stopped. The top chief spat out a few quick questions to the Indian translator who related them to Nielson.

"He wants to know how you know about the

challenge of the gods," the clearly terrified Nielson said. "How the hell *did* you know, anyway?"

"All tribes the world over have challenges — ways to avoid certain death. It's like an escape valve for the common man — some method in lieu of a system of law for him to have at least a shot at getting out of trouble. I took a chance — what'd we have to lose? But don't tell him that. Tell him," Rock said, pausing, glancing over at the wizened old face that glared at him suspiciously, wondering what all the talk was about, "tell him that I have great magic, powerful explosive magic. That I *made* the volcano erupt because I wanted it to. That how else could we have come from that direction unless I was a top magic man."

Nielson looked confused.

"Just tell him all that — don't worry how it sounds."

The nervous Freefighter made his hand-signals again — he and his Sioux counterpart quickly understanding one another's gestures now and communicating in seconds with a flurry of fingers and palms. Rockson kept his eyes fixed firmly on the top chief's face to see his reaction as the words were translated. The prune-faced man's pupils seemed to dilate for a second as if from fear — but the old man had been through too many poker games of nerves with his own upstarts and would-be assassins to buckle under Rockson's gaze. He looked straight back, twin orbs of shiny black beneath folds of red leathery skin focused on Rockson without a flicker of emotion. But the Doomsday Warrior knew that he had affected him — knew that magic, superstition, their fears of things they didn't understand were his ace in the hole.

And that he would play it to the hilt.

As the top chiefs conferred, arguing back and forth, Rockson lifted his bound arms to the sky and yelled out his own incantations to the white man's gods. The Indians stopped talking for a moment and looked on in consternation.

"How much woooood
Could a woodchuck chuuuuck
If a woodchuck couullld
Chuck wood, chuck wood, chuck wood."

Rockson sang in long, drawn-out vowels, snapping his teeth together hard on all the consonants so that the entire thing sounded like an angry call to the demons of the darkness. The gulley-faced chief seemed to sink even deeper into the folds of animal skin that surrounded him. Rockson kept on with the mad chantings, stamping his feet up and down in a makeshift dance, swinging his tied hands around in front of him in wide concentric circles. The other Freefighters, though tied and marked for imminent death, could barely suppress their laughter at the Doomsday Warrior's remarkable theatrics.

The chiefs conferred again—all of them looking worried now—and then apparently came to some sort of decision as they stopped talking and stared at Rockson as if he was a hideous bug that had crawled out from under a slime-coated log. The translator walked back over to Nielson and the two went at it again with gusto. After a minute, Nielson turned to the Doomsday Warrior.

"Well, you've got your wish, Rock. The Challenge-of-the-Buffalo, as they call it. Whatever it is—you're going to get a chance to find out right now."

"Thanks, Nielson—whatever happens," Rock said softly. "You did good, real good."

"Rock, one more thing. I think they're a little afraid of you now. That woodchuck tune and your praying stuff stirred 'em up. Some of the sign language that the translator was using had connotations of—madman from the skies or lunatic eagle with wings of fire—I don't know—something. But whatever you're doing—is definitely psyching 'em out."

Four hulking braves appeared and hoisted Rockson, two on a side, and carried him to the center of a circle about fifty feet in diameter where they deposited him roughly on the dirt. The Doomsday Warrior looked around curiously, wondering just what the hell was going to happen next—and started to work his hands completely free so he could take on whatever it was. From out of a thirty-foot-high teepee with the skulls of buffalo surrounding it like a fence came a whole crew of the biggest of the young braves—and over the tops of their bodies—full buffalo heads with eyes, fur, and horns as long and sharp as daggers. The ten Sioux holding aloft bludgeon-sized tomahawks, quickly came over to the circle and lined up on the perimeter until they were evenly distributed around Rockson. Then they came in slowly, ever closer, for the kill.

The Doomsday Warrior gulped, looked up for a split second toward the sky—launching an appeal to a—hopefully—compassionate God who he hoped was in a good mood today—and wriggled his flexible mutant's-hands free of the leather thongs. This was not going to be easy. No—he couldn't doubt himself, couldn't think about getting them all at once. Just one at a time, that's all—one at a time. Or so the little pep talk he gave himself went. Until the entire group came charging forward, their buffalo heads pointed straight ahead, polished curved horns reaching out a yard or more toward his flesh, tomahawks flailing.

Rock shot between two of them, kicking the legs out from under one brave as he went and slamming the buffalo head down onto the rock-strewn ground with a thump. He slid behind the body and down, so that though the crowd of hundreds of Sioux who stood around could see where he was, for just a few seconds the horned braves who had sped forward, butting at the air trying to rip the white-skin, didn't realize that their prey had ducked them. Rock slid his hands down the groaning Indian's side and felt a handle. He ripped it free and, with something approaching joy, saw that it was a long double-edged hunting knife, solid and as well-balanced as a small sword. Someone up there liked him, or at least wanted to draw the contest out a bit. He jabbed the fallen brave; a deep twisting blow. *One down*. The Doomsday Warrior thought for the sheerest second of dashing over to free his imprisoned team—but quickly took in the mob of Indians standing all around the open field in the center of the encampment—and thought better of it. They'd rip him apart like a snarlizard on a deer. There was only one way he, or the others were going to get out of this damned thing alive. That was by killing every one of the bastards—who were just realizing that their prey had vanished. Before the 9 warriors left standing could turn, Rockson ran several yards toward the tightened circle and attacked from the rear. He lunged almost with a fencing motion and plunged the sixteen-inch knife into the back of the closest Sioux brave. The razor-sharp sliver of steel slid into the flesh like butter and severed one side of the man's spinal cord. He fell to the ground as if he'd never been born, unable to move a muscle though his eyes still twisted and turned inside the paralyzed skull as if searching frantically for memories of the life he was about to leave. The buffalo heads were obviously impeding their vision. There was a chance after all.

The rest, realizing their charge had missed its mark, turned to find the crazy white man who had dared to challenge the horns of the buffalo—from which no man in their history had escaped. Rock caught the closest brave, who leapt madly forward trying to split Rock's mutant-skull with his tomahawk. With a snapping roundhouse kick as the Indian swung and he ducked, Rock's booted foot slammed into the brave's groin, squashing the testicles to a bloody pancake. No need to kill him, he was down for the duration, scrunched up in foetal position.

The Doomsday Warrior suddenly felt a stabbing pain in his back and spun around just in time to avoid the full thrust of one of the ivory-colored horns that were being head-speared at him. The bearer of the murderous tidings flew past, taking some of Rock's blood away on the sharp prong. But as the Sioux dug his feet into the ground to turn, the Doomsday Warrior's blade descended through the flea-bitten flap of buffalo hide over his shoulders and into the brave's neck. Again the knife's aim was true. The top side of the double-edged weapon cut along the throat's nerve ganglia, the blood vessels. Rock pulled the knife out, dripping red. The Indian was stopped like a pickup truck out of gas and slammed forward, the buffalo helmet falling off to reveal the man's head hanging by spurting arteries, in his neck a gaping hole of bloody muscle. Hands over his throat, the Sioux flopped around the sandy circle like a fish out of water, no longer a threat to anyone, gargling blood as he waited to die.

Rock thought for a moment of grabbing the fallen buffalo mask which lay at his feet. But he had no idea of how to use the thing—besides, it would only slow him down. As deadly as the long horns were, wearing the masks was obviously cutting the Indians' mobility and vision considerably. Presumably no one who had faced them before had been able to move fast enough to avoid those goring horns. And once securely impaled—it was all over. Speed—that was all he had—and the ability to fight like a demon. A pair of horns came at him from the side, catching Rockson slightly off balance. Seeing he had no time, the Doomsday Warrior, instead of trying to evade the attack, took it head on. As the Sioux slammed into his belly, Rock eased back and grabbed hold of both horns with an iron grip. Using the brave's own mass and speed, Rockson let himself be pushed backwards. He hit the ground on his back and pulled the Indian forward and over, kicking up into the man's chest with all his might. Buffalo head and owner went flying past, landing two yards behind Rock where the Indian tried to pull free of the now-confining weapon.

Rockson didn't give him time, leaping with a heave of his steel thighs toward the stunned brave. As he landed alongside the man, another set of sunbaked buffalo horns came out of the center of the circle toward him with the speed of a real bison. Rockson shot his knife arm straight out to meet the skull of the oncoming locomotive dead on between the eyes. He brought the heel of his boot down on the back of the neck of the brave who was just emerging from his helmet. The neck snapped with the sickening sound of a chicken bone cracking in two. At the same instant, his blood-coated blade sank deep into animal skull and then the human one beneath it. The case-hardened steel ripped through the Indian's head and deep into the brain below, slicing memory into madness and life into death in the twist of a wrist. "W-o-o-d-chuck, chuck-chuck," Rock chanted, remembering Nielson said it seemed to make them worried. The remaining buffalo-heads froze in place, even backed off a bit. The whopping crowd grew silent.

He wiped his eyes with his sleeve as he walked slowly backwards, in a low-legged horse stance, ready for the next attack. The entire battle had lasted under thirty seconds so far, and Rock had no idea how many he'd taken out. But as he wheeled, he saw only four of the huge heads confronting him from the sides of the circle. He realized that the odds were coming round. Maybe he'd even live. The wound in his side sent a shiver of sharp pain through his nerves and Rockson winced as he felt a thin stream of blood oozing down his leg and into his boot, making it simultaneously sticky and slippery inside. He used the bolt of pure pain to charge him up, to push his adrenaline to even higher levels, his senses to a peak. Then he waited for *them* to make the next move.

The four buffalo heads looked around at each other, alarmed to see how many the mad magic of the white man had killed. None had ever done so well before. For the first time in their entire lives the four knew real heart-pounding fear, as they realized that their own lives were suddenly very much at stake. They yelled what Rockson took to be words of macho encouragement to one another and then started forward, trying to fence him in and end it with the piercing of eight horns into his flesh. But Rock had trained for years in fighting multiple opponents. For the more there were of them, the more their movements—not his—were confined. The more chance there was for an opening.

He saw it. As they closed to within feet of him, one of the braves stumbled slightly and went half-down on one knee. In the batting of an eyelash the Doomsday Warrior reached the man in a single stride and jumped right over him, just clearing the horns as they came up in a murderous thrust at his stomach. Rock came down on his feet just behind the Indian and turned without even coming to a stop, jumping up onto the buffalo-man's back.

Now he had a mount, the Doomsday Warrior thought with a flicker of amusement. And he'd use it. Wrapping his left arm around the brave's throat, he held the knife out with the other and jabbed into the man's lower back. The Indian shot forward as if a hot poker was up his ass, trying to escape the tip of the blade which Rock had stabbed in only an inch or so, to avoid mortally wounding his human horse. The scampering Sioux crashed right into the masked brave coming in the opposite direction, and as they collided Rockson took the opportunity to swing the knife under and up, coming into the nearest Sioux's throat. From the gurgling sounds that issued from the warrior's mouth, Rock knew that he had struck paydirt and pulled the blade out again as he sensed the presence of an attacker just behind him. "Wood-chuck-chuck-chuck," he chanted.

Using his stabbing double-edged reins, Rock plunged the blade deep into the right leg of the Indian who was unwillingly carrying him. The man screamed and fell to that side, spinning around.

Rock and his captive mount fell to the ground in a heap as the attacker's lunging horns sliced into the air that Rockson had just been occupying.

"Bye, bye, pal," the Doomsday Warrior whispered into the ear of the steed who had served him so loyally for nine seconds, and brought the knife down right into the top of the buffalo mask, striking something that cracked, shuddered and then was still. He jumped to his feet as one of the masked Indians leaped into the air at full speed and headed toward Rock's chest like a hairy horned missile. There was no chance to get away, so the Doomsday Warrior stood his ground, turning his upper body and hips just enough so the shooting star of fur missed him by inches. He remembered what Chen had always told him when they sparred together back in Century City: "Don't commit yourself in the air. 'Cause once you're launched, you're just a slow-flying duck waiting to be shot down." The Indian flying by alongside of Rockson had apparently never heard that advice. And he never would. Rock held the knife straight up dead-center of the airborne body. The tip of the blade caught the Indian first at the top of his nose. It dug in and sliced a furrow that ran the full length of the Sioux's body as he flew by, a plowed field of flesh from which a crop of blood and lungs instantly grew. He came down several yards past Rockson, sliding into the dusty ground like a 707 coming in for a belly landing. He slid, leaving a trail of red foam on the runway, came to a complete stop, and didn't move again.

Rock turned, searching for more Sioux attackers, but could find only dead or barely moving bodies around the now blood-soaked ritual circle of combat. Then he saw the last of them at the far side of the circle. He had thrown his buffalo mask from his head and shoulders and was backing away from Rockson, screaming something out in Sioux as the crowd around them both joined in, cursing and spitting at the treacherous foe who had vanquished their best braves unfairly, with use of a black-magic chant. The last fighter was handed a bow and an arrow, which he quickly fitted into the cord. Rock couldn't understand the Indian's mouthings but he knew roughly what the intent was: "If you think you won, forget it, man! I'll kill you even though it is against the rules." The brave slowly raised the bow, and pulled the string back as the smile on his desert-hardened face grew wider and wider.

Seeing that there was no referee for Rockson to appeal to about the disobeying of Challenge-of-the-

189

Buffalo regulations, the Doomsday Warrior decided to make the judgment call on his own. He flipped the knife in the air and caught the blade. Before the brave even saw the motion, Rock brought the knife up to his shoulder, balancing it exactly two thirds of the way down the dripping red steel, and released it with all his throwing strength. The blade spiraled forward, spinning end over end across the Indian graveyard that Rockson had just created below it. The Indian's smile began to vanish as he saw it coming. But the agent-of-death was already halfway across. Frantically the brave swung his bow up and pulled the string the rest of the way back to his ear. Like a bird coming home to the nest, the blade seemed to veer infinitesimally to the right and slammed claws first into the Indian's right eye. The hand released the arrow, which flew wildly off, missing Rockson by yards. The Indian clamped both hands over his face, the knife sticking through the eye socket, buried nearly to the hilt and poking out the back of the warrior's skull. Without making a sound, he toppled forward onto his face.

Rock stood up, relaxing his super-tense muscles, and looked around him. The place was a butchershop of human flesh. With the buffalo heads lying around the bodies of their previous owners, the entire scene had a surreal look to it. As if it was a monument, a Stonehenge of animal and human masks dedicated to a ceremonial proposition that any and all mortals can die at any second.

Chapter Fourteen

Rockson was called before the assembled chiefs as the Sioux translator and Nielson went at it again like Martians trying to speak Greek to one another. The feathered top brass looked positively sickened at the outcome, their lips trembling, their eyes dark and filled with raging fire at the man who had destroyed their champs. Shom-ga-na nervously stepped forward to translate, hoping Rockson wouldn't chant the death-chant anymore.

"Rock, you bastard," Nielson said, turning to his commander. "You won. They say you are the one who it was prophesied would come. The Buffalo Hunter, the one capable of destroying their masked marauders there. They don't like the idea but apparently—you're the big cheese here now. You won the place." The Sioux translator grunted to catch Nielson's attention and gave him another flurried hand-fan of messages from Chief Bright Sun.

"They want to know what you want to do with the village, with the women. Where they should go to be imprisoned; if they are to be your slaves."

Rockson waved his hand in disgust at the idea and

nodded to the top chief, who let a grimace of a smile twist across his stone face before it settled into its dark prune-folds once again.

"Tell them—especially tell the top banana here, who looks like he's about to have a heart attack—that I'm not in the least bit interested in taking over this development. That he's still the boss and that all we want to do is get the hell out of here." Nielson translated the message to the sub-chief whose face grew brighter and brighter with each thought that was communicated. He turned and barked out the words to the chiefs who all leaned forward on their royal deerskin and buffalo-hide divans, their faces showing little flickers of relief that vanished instantly. The top man spoke and Nielson interpreted the results.

"The chief says you are free to go. They will give you all the supplies you want—and none of your flock will be harmed. He says he hopes they haven't in their stupidity of your godly ways offended you."

"Tell them I am sorry that so many of their strong young men had to die. That we are all Americans—and no matter what our inglorious past together, we can only face the future as brothers or we will die alone, atomized into impotent little units that will be destroyed by the invading tribes of Russians."

Nielson translated the words into sign language, and then the response from the chief.

"He says the word of the Buffalo Slayer is law now. They will no longer kill Americans—only Russians—only those who wear the Red Star uniform." Rockson bowed to the chief and then stood tall, snapping out a crisp U.S. Army-style salute. Gulley Face returned the gesture.

The Freefighters' weapons and 'brids were returned to them loaded up with supplies of fresh fruit, meat, and replenished gourds of water. They marched through the central sandy square past the now totally silent and bowing New-Sioux, who watched Rockson with eyes filled with both fear and worship. A man so strong would have been great, powerful, unbeatable magic for their tribe. And Rock swore he saw a twinkle in the eye of the old chief, thanking him for splitting the scene—and for leaving the power structure intact.

They rode straight north for 16 hours without stopping, just slowing every hour for five minutes to walk, at which time the 'brids were given water via a long curved tube from a gourd—Indian canteens—held in the arms of their riders. With good weather and no spy drones around to signal their passage, the force made excellent time—finding themselves at last within miles of their rendezvous point with the American army of several thousand men who—if all was going according to plan—were in the final stages of setting up the invasion of Fort Minsk from the woods that surrounded it.

They came to the south end of the thick forest and tramped into it, moving slowly as the branches grew lower. Rockson was just beginning to wonder where the hell his men were and if something had gone wrong when he heard the heart-warming challenge.

"Halt—give the password," a hidden voice intoned from the maze of leaves to the right of them. Rock knew that at least a dozen guns were trained on them right that second. He moved slowly so as not to spook any jittery fingers.

193

"Silver threads—" Rock said loudly, cupping his hands over his mouth.

"Among the gold." The voice cried back, as several figures dropped from the limbs around them.

"Rockson," the head of the guard detail exclaimed, "where the hell you been? All the top brass been, pardon the expression, crapping in their pants waiting for you to get here. The attack is due to begin in 24 hours and—"

"Well, let's not waste any more time then, pal," Rock said, slapping the unshaven, baggy-eyed Freefighter on the back. "Ran into a few sideshows on the road. You know how it is." The entire team breathed a sigh of relief that they had actually made it as the journey had given them a little more action than usual. For the first time in days their stomach muscles relaxed and their lungs filled completely with air as they realized, unwinding, that they had been coiled as tight as springs about to snap.

They were led a mile through the woods, the immense Fort Minsk occasionally visible through the branches to the north of them, until they came to a camp set up beneath the trees—tents and hammocks strung along their lower limbs. The whole thing was somewhat constricting to get around in but necessary because of their proximity to the KGB-held fortress and the occasional chopper that flew overhead. The rest of the team headed for showers, fresh clothes, and food while Rock just stopped to grab a cup of steaming black coffee from one of the many coffee-pots that sat on no-smoke pellet stoves. He walked to the command post, a rectangular camouflage-patterned tent that ran fifty feet long but, because of the

194

many branches overhead, was only about six feet high. He pushed aside the front flaps. A meeting consisting of Century City's top ten military men was in heated progress, with General Hastings, the white-haired chief of staff, banging his fist down on the log table they'd lashed together, which was covered with maps and battle plans.

"Rock," Hastings said, stopping whatever he was about to extrapolate on in mid-sentence. The military brass, somehow managing to be well-groomed, their uniforms pressed and straight, all looked up. Their eyes focused on Rockson's face as if he was a mixture of the Almighty savior and a warthog all rolled into one. The military leaders of the subterranean city had always had an uneasy alliance with Rockson. Although highly successful in his military planning and maneuvers in the past—and therefore virtually immune to criticism—the man irked them in a thousand different ways. He never wore a real uniform, never saluted, or followed any of the customary procedures and rules that were the glue of any man's army. He never had his special men march parade drill, wear regulation combat gear, or do army calisthenics or workouts of any kind. He just wasn't—an army man. Yet, as the living symbol of America's resistance, he had an official say and even ultimate veto over all major military moves. Not that he pulled rank—of that they were grateful. If anything, the man seemed most content when off on a mission of his own, by himself or just his five-man team. Perhaps deep down inside the hearts of each of the brass was a wish to be like Rockson—a born and perfect warrior. But only their jealous eyes expressed the feeling, as their mouths welcomed him to the meeting.

Rock waved his hands, not wanting to go through all the formalities. "Please, please, gentlemen. Just pretend I'm not here and continue with your discussion. You can fill me in as you go along."

"Well, Rock," Hastings went on, "we were just discussing —"

"Arguing," General Spokes yelled out with a hard laugh.

"Arguing," Hastings agreed, "about the best battle formation. We really haven't had too much experience in laying waste a whole fortress. As you know, most of our military expeditions since Century City was founded have been hitting convoys, smaller bases. Strike-destroy-split. So none of us, in all honesty, has been really sure how to proceed. We dug up some old siege booklets from the Military Library back at Century City but they're obsolete for a number of reasons." Rock listened intently, nursing the coffee down to the bitter grounds, wishing there was more.

"So we were just dis — arguing about whether to send all our forces against one wall — mortar, machine gun, infantrymen — and try to bring it down. Or to attack all four sides, weaken their inner forces, disperse them and try to move in fast with a mobile commando unit and get inside. I must say I favor the one-wall scenario," General Hastings added, wanting to get his point over first. "We know that Minsk is filled with heavy artillery up on the walls — auto-fire machine guns, rocket racks — the works. Assuming Killov and his men can handle what they've got there — then they've got a hundred times the firepower that we do. Intel Chief Rath convinced the Century City council to cut by 60% the number of Freefighters the city would send here.

"Damn," muttered Rockson. "That bastard Rath . . ."

"The way I see it then," the General continued, "our only chance is to just keep blasting every goddamned bit of fire we possess on one section of one wall—rip it apart—and then get our asses in there fast." The portly but physically strong-as-a-bull general finished and sat back, trying to gauge Rockson's reaction.

"Sounds as good as anything I could come up with," Rock said matter-of-factly, adding, "is there any coffee around here?"

"Orderly, orderly," Hastings sputtered impatiently to one of several uniformed soldiers standing around the log table. "Bring two pots of coffee and some food. On the double." The trooper ran out and returned with impossible quickness with the required items. Rock couldn't help himself, as his growling stomach demanded it, and began stuffing his mouth with the various rolls, pastries, and assorted doughy items that were brought in as the generals continued their heated debate—each side of the argument sure that only their plan would bring victory, and the adoption of the other's position—total, humiliating defeat.

Before they could make a final decision—and before Rockson had cleaned off the food tray, one of the outer forest guards came rushing right through the flaps of the tent where he hit into the edge of the branch-lashed table, sending it and himself flying over sideways onto the dirt.

"Sirs, sirs, sorry," heaved out the young Freefighter through dry lips, gasping for air, his face bright as an apple in October. "Just run a mile 'out stopping," explained the strapping lad, barely out of his teens. "'Cause some people showed up at the southeast woods—and sirs, thy—they—they—" He couldn't seem to find the words and every man in the room stared down incredulously at his wild-eyed face.

"They *what*?" Hastings asked impatiently.

"They're weird, sirs, *weird*."

Chapter Fifteen

As Rockson came out of the southeast perimeter of the trees around the Freefighter camp, he could see immediately that the kid had been telling the truth. Weird wasn't the half of it. For coming off the plains in a fifty-yard-wide line that stretched back a good mile was an army that looked like it was out of The Arabian Nights. At the front—the cavalry riding tall black steeds that looked more like the horses of the 20th century than the Freefighters' own mutated 'brids. Atop them, carrying their fighting flags and banners, sat white-robed warriors with long pointed beards and with swords at their sides. Behind them came the infantry, long lines of turbaned troops bearing an odd assortment of both primitive and modern weapons—machine guns and bows, lances and bazookas. And far in the rear, Rock could see from atop Snorter, were men pushing immense wooden structures on roughly hewn wheels. There were ropes and pulleys and levers all over the damned things, but for the life of him the Doomsday Warrior couldn't imagine what they were.

The two riders at the very front of the army drew

closer and Rock saw that they were shielded from the sun by men riding alongside them holding large silk umbrellas. The men's eyes were fierce, countless diamonds, sapphires, and blood-red rubies burning on their robes and turbans, set afire by the stabbing rays of the afternoon sun. They made quite an impressive picture, and Rockson knew by the calmness of their demeanor and the tornado just behind their eyes that they were fighters of the highest order—men who had killed many times.

"Bow, cur!" one of the riders spat out at Rock in perfect English as he and his bejeweled companion pulled to a stop before him. The entire army slowed down and the men began marching in place without missing a step. The fierce brown eyes stared down at Rockson.

"No thanks," Rock said, spitting a mouthful of coffee grounds down next to his 'brid. "I don't even bow to kings and holy men. What are you?"

"A general, fool," the older of the two barked down, his eyes beginning to spark with fury. "And by what odious appellation are you known to those with the misfortune to be in your company?"

"Ted Rockson, an officer of the Army of the Re-United States of America."

The mounted Sikh general seemed to turn to stone for a moment as his mind took in the words, and he looked at his partner with a quizzical glance as if wondering whether to believe it. The younger man looked down at Rockson with a little less antagonism and asked, "What can never be allowed to be opened?"

"The Seventh Seal, for within it lies ten thousand

years of darkness," Rock replied, giving the response that he and Rahallah had agreed to over the phone, so that Vassily's forces would be able to identify themselves. Vassily's Sikh army had arrived.

"*You* are Rockson?" the silver-bearded Sikh fighter asked with barely disguised scorn. "I am General Sikh Panchali, and this," he said, pointing a lazy finger to his right, "is General Ragdar. We are the Royal Indian Sikh Army under the personal orders of Premier Vassily to join with your—" he looked around and sniffed the air as if he found something not to his liking, "army, which I am afraid I do not see anywhere. Nor do I see lines of troops to greet us, or buglers signaling our arrival. This is not how we do things in the Asias! The ritual of preparing for battle is as important as the execution of it. I must say, I *am* disappointed."

"Sorry, General," Rock said with a click of the tongue and a quick smile. "We Americans never were much for all that 'God-save-the-Queen' stuff—but we're kick-ass fighters. I promise you that. How the hell did you get here, anyway—just marching along out of nowhere?"

"Our fleet of transport planes touched down about fifty miles east of here," Ragdar said, folding his wide-sleeved arms across his chest, emeralds sewn along the seams glistening like little tongues of green fire every time he moved. "So we marched."

"Through the wastelands?" Rock asked, remembering snakes and such.

"Compared to the mountainous regions we have fought in," Ragdar said, "your wastelands, as you call them, are like an oasis to us. We come from the least

201

hospitable terrain on this planet, General Rockson. Landscapes that can only be likened to the dark side of the moon."

"And your English, you speak so—"

"Of course we do," General Panchali butted in, snapping loudly at Rockson. "Every Sikh officer speaks at least four languages, many five, even six. English is one. I must apologize for Sikh Panchali," the younger Sikh said. "He has been killing men for too long to remember how to greet them, I am afraid. But for both of us I give greetings and prayers for success at our joint venture."

"I hate to bring it up," Rock exclaimed, looking past the two men at their army spread out across a mile of terrain, totally exposed to air attack. "But don't you think your men should have better cover, should get into the woods, should—"

"We do not fear attack," General Panchali said loudly, motioning for his umbrella bearer to put the thing away as the sun was dropping behind the trees and its direct light and heat were dissipating. "In the hundred years my army has been in existence—no one has defeated us, General Rockson. Those who dare attack us are welcome to try. We run from no man." He turned on his gilded saddle and gave a simple head motion to his subordinate officers, who immediately ordered the troops to dismount and make camp right there in the open, just feet from the sheltering forest. Rockson shook his head in disbelief.

"And now," Ragdar said with a smile, "you must inform us of your battle plans so that we may begin briefing our men."

"Well, to be honest with you," Rock said, feeling

foolish, "we'd been wondering just that thing ourselves. You wouldn't have any ideas, would you?"

"You want to take the fort," Panchali said, snapping his fingers together. "It is simple. We are experts of siege, of laying waste to 'indestructible' structures. You have undoubtedly heard of our exploits, our conquering of the entire Tibetan armies, our taking of whole nations—even over here." The silver-bearded general sat back on his wide elephant-skin saddle and waited for the praise to pour on.

"Sorry to disappoint you," Rock responded, "but we don't get much in the way of international newspapers or the evening world news on television—so not too many of us are that well informed on world events. But I'm sure we'd all be fascinated to hear about your exploits. Your place—or mine—for the get-together?"

That night Rockson got his stated desire and more—as the Freefighters came to a banquet thrown by the two Sikh generals. Rock brought Kim, Rona, and the Rock team along with fifty or so Freefighting officers who would be leading the rest of the American men into battle. Rock and the top staff agreed that it would be wise for at least the officers of the two armies to meet and get a nodding acquaintance—since they would be fighting for their lives together within 24 hours. The Sikh generals, anxious to show off their brand of "having one over for a bite," had erected a long brightly colored tent with high billowing silk walls and banners intricately embroidered with lions' heads and dragons. Inside, the tent was like a dream of Asian jaded luxury—long tables filled with fruit, steaming platters of meat and fish, decanters and bottles of multicolored liquids carried around on silver platters by black-robed servants, musicians playing rhythmic but alien-sounding music that followed no tonal system Rockson had ever heard on long, curved stringed instruments.

The guests of honor were led in and to their places on immense, overstuffed satin pillows that lay around thick rugs which covered the entire tented ground.

"Excellent, excellent," Ragdar said from his own pillow. Two young veiled, but bare midriffed women on either side of him were feeding grapes into his mouth. "So glad you could all come." Rockson sat on one side of him as Kim and Rona each tried to grab the pillow closest to the Doomsday Warrior. Chen, Detroit, McCaughlin, and Archer all walked slowly around the place, gawking at the extravagant silks and weavings and gilded cow heads that hung on the tent walls. And the food—mountains of it, a feast one could only imagine in a dream. Vassily's impromptu airlift of men and supplies must have been massive. But what about quality?

But when they cut into the rare roast beef, bit into the yogurt and honey sparrow eggs, they knew it was real.

"Where the hell did you get all this stuff?" Rock asked after he'd taken a few bites. "These things don't grow around here."

"General Rockson," Sikh Panchali said as a young woman covered in gossamer pink veils and bracelets fed him bite-sized portions of partridge pâté and truffles, "one thing our fighting forefathers learned very early in the formation of the Royal Sikh Army was to have the best of everything. It is only worth dying when one's *life* is rich and full. Thus—we carry out Moscow's orders and we are rewarded with the finest things that a man can have. One entire transport plane was filled with boxes and refrigerated containers of our culinary needs."

"This is the way to fight a war," Rona said, stuffing her mouth with the turtle eggs in chocolate sauce, which for some not-inexplicable reason she found irresistible.

"Why can't we bring lunchboxes like this along on all our missions?" Detroit yelled from across the table, his own plate piled so high that things were slipping off as he ate. The rest of the team dug in with much enthusiasm, each eating like it was their last meal—which for some would be the case. Archer wolfed down whole platefuls in a bite and reached for whatever was closest as it passed by with a long pronged serving fork.

Panchali clapped his hands after a few minutes and a line of dancing girls came out dressed in gossamer veils, which barely concealed their charms. They began undulating, insinuating their rather attractive musculature directly under the eyes of Ted Rockson and batting their moist doe-like eyes at him. Rona and Kim both coughed loudly and stared at the Doomsday Warrior with green rising in their eyes. This man had it too good!

"If you so much as look at once inch of those— those women," Kim sputtered, "I'll put .45's in both your eyes." She banged her small fist down on the table, making a plate of creamed onions bounce slightly and several of the little grease balls rolled onto the silk tablecloth. Rock kept his eyes on his food. Rona leaned over and buttered his rolls, showing as much cleavage in her mostly open shirt as the dancing girls.

"You see," Ragdar said, smiling at Rockson, whom he could see was truly impressed by the display of wealth. "The ancients knew it well. All their fighting men—early Egyptians, the Greeks, Caesar's, Alexander the Great's—they always made war in style with feasts and women along the way. Why must a combat soldier *suffer* his hours when he is not fighting? He suffers enough in battle. Really, it is such an outmoded concept! I am surprised at your backwardness in such matters!" The Sikh general scolded Rockson in a mocking fashion with his ringed finger.

"You're goddamned right there's 'backwardness' in such matters," Rona said loudly. "This is the United States you're in now, pal. And our faiths, our traditions—our everything dictate that we do things our own way. And that means no dancing girls. The Freefighters got *us*." She smiled sweetly at Rockson and then at Kim and folded her hands across her ample chest, satisfied that she'd at least said her piece.

Panchali and Ragdar gathered the top Freefighter commanders around the dinner table, once the feast had finished. Panchali swept the dishes, silverware, and glasses from the table with a dramatic flourish, sending the contents crashing onto the floor where they were attended to by a cluster of efficient servants. Panchali then pulled out a large pencil-drawn map and unfolded it on top of the table.

"This is a map of the fortress," the Sikh general said, probing his teeth with a golden toothpick. "You can see it from all four flanks."

"That's remarkable," Chen intoned as he slowly sipped some after-dinner plum brandy. "Where did you dig that up?"

"We make our own maps, General Chen," Ragdar said with a quick good-humored laugh. They'd taken to calling Rockson and his top five men "General," unable to conceive that leaders of such numbers of troops could be of anything less than of that august ranking. "The moment we arrived, our cartographers were in the field making drawings, using surveying equipment to get the exact distances and dimensions of Minsk."

"Yes, General Rockson," Panchali interjected, his face glowing with excitement for the first time that evening—as the subject was war. "We have found through costly experience that the more one knows *exactly* what the enemy's strengths and weaknesses are, where his highest walls and lowest walls are, their makeup, the more one knows everything about him— as in making a fine piece of carpentry—the results will come out perfect if the measurements are correct. War is a science to us, General, not a game of chance."

Rockson was impressed as the generals went over the maps, which showed the approaches to the outer walls, the entrances that must be breached. Whatever their kingly airs, the Sikh men seemed to be the real thing—military strategists who knew how to kill better than the enemy. The Doomsday Warrior paid close attention to their words, their concepts. There was a lot to be learned from men such as these, steeped in siege-warfare.

"So you see, it's really absurdly simple," Panchali went on, holding a long carving knife he had picked up from the table and using it as a pointer along the map. "We simply create diversionary attacks on the south, east, and west walls but concentrate our *main* attack on the north wall—the least protected because of the inhospitable terrain. But what is thought uncrossable by Russian planners is, for us, an eight-lane super-highway. Once the north wall is taken, cavalry and infantry will attack, sending all forces into the fortress. They have been instructed to kill only KGB and release Red troops. We are, as you can see," Panchali said, sitting back with a smug look, "completely prepared. The situation is in hand."

"And what of *my* men?" Rockson asked, leaning forward. "Where do we come in?"

"Oh really," Panchali said with a bemused look. "We're used to doing it alone. At least until the first fighters open the gates, I think you'd just be in the way."

Rockson didn't show a flicker of anger and froze Chen and Detroit, whom he saw start to rise in fury, with but a single glance.

"I don't think you understand, General," Rockson said coolly. "We're in this together. We asked for you to come here to *help* us. I don't mind if you run the show, since you seem to know what you're doing strategically—but my men *are* to be in on every phase of it. You may be great fighters—but I daresay you've never fought the KGB or Colonel Killov over there in Asia. And as dangerous and fierce as those you faced may have been, I have a feeling your men will be glad there are some American kick-ass Freefighters along to point a few things out."

"I just don't think—" Panchali began again, his eyes rolling up, but Ragdar cut him off.

"I'm sure what my co-general means," the younger and more diplomatic Sikh said, "is that we'd be glad to have you along as long as our men and your men know just how to place themselves so they won't accidentally injure one another. Isn't that right, brother?" Ragdar asked, looking at Panchali with a don't-fuck-with-me-now expression.

"Of course, of course," Panchali blurted out, knowing that he easily enraged others and that he'd be better off letting the younger man take care of it all. "You must excuse me, Generals—I am so clumsy with words sometimes, a soldier who sometimes forgets the social niceties that allow for interaction between men."

"At any rate," Ragdar went on as Panchali sat back in his chair and drank a dark blue liquid from a crystal goblet, "we attack at midnight tomorrow and—"

"And your equipment—those huge wooden things," Rock asked, "what are they, how—"

"Please, General Rockson," Ragdar said, snapping his fingers for more wine, "it's so difficult to explain it all—you'll see tomorrow night. A battle, as they say, is worth a thousand military manuals. As we move into position, you'll see it all." He looked at Rockson. "If you want, pick your own team and come in with the first of us!"

"I propose a toast," the black Freefighter said with the beginnings of an idiotic drunken smile, "to our fine Asian fighters — whoever they killed in the past — we thank them for coming to our aid." The Free-fighters raised their glasses in salute and downed their drinks.

"And my turn," Ragdar said, as a servant filled his glass with a golden syrupy liqueur. "A toast to fighting men everywhere — whatever their rank or army. To the combat soldiers of history." They all raised their glasses once again and happily downed the contents.

Before the others could respond, Ragdar pulled another glass, already filled, from the table and turned toward Rona and Kim. They were starting to loosen up a little now that their third shots of booze had hit their stomachs.

"And may I say," the young, quite handsome if rather large-nosed, Sikh pronounced with a twinkle in both eyes as he looked at the Freefighter females, "that the American rebel army possesses some of the most beautiful women I have ever seen in my travels around a good portion of this planet. To General Rona and General Kim." He smiled the sexiest smile he could manage, directing it with all his dark-eyed male power at the two and swallowed the liquor gustily. Both women blushed, not daring to look either at Ragdar or Rockson, and quaffed theirs in a single gulp too.

With that it was off to the races with toasts by every man sitting around the table. There were toasts to great generals of the past, toasts to battles, toasts to presidents. After several more rounds, it was toasts to movie stars of the pre-nuke days, and then toasts to the banquet's attendees, one by one.

If the intention of the feast was to get the top ranks of the two armies better acquainted, it was working. Dancing contests erupted, arm wrestling championships, and boxing matches as they went at it, testing each other's skills, each other's mettle as men. And being amazed at each nation's prowess.

And as the men's macho came out, so did the women's machisma.

There's something about knowing you might die on the morrow and consuming five, six, or seven high-proof drinks that sends one's inhibitions into hibernation. As some of the men gyrated atop other tables, Rona took off her heavy boots jumped up right in front of Rockson, kicked the military maps aside, and began dancing, giving her lover obvious and wicked looks. Not to be outdone, Kim removed her clod-hoppers, leaped up and joined her several feet away. Both of them began spinning around as Freefighters and Sikh officers around the room joined in clapping hands in time to the now-pulsing odd but sensual music that had reached the decibel level of a symphonic orchestra.

Drinks were handed to the women and they gulped them down, while laughing, twirling around. Kim was the first to remove an article of clothing, her pants falling down, she stepped out of them. Rockson didn't know whether to stop her.

Kim taunted, "Ashamed of *your* body, Rona?"

Rona tore off her freshly ironed fatigue jacket. The alcohol, the dizziness, the rising chorus of whistles pushed them both to heights they would never ordinarily have reached. But now, in a whirlwind of challenges back and forth, they stripped off one garment after another until both of them danced atop the table in just panties, swinging their bodies around like the dancing girls who continued to undulate through the crowd, diamonds in their navels and adorning the tips of their breasts, making the three points shine like shimmering stars in the oil-lamps' lights.

Rock's own brain was somewhere on the floor. He hadn't drunk this much for years, but was already beyond the ability to judge or care. Somewhere in his head he knew they would regret this tomorrow—but now was a swirling fog of laughter, he had a stupid feeling that everything was fine. He watched the two near-naked women, the two bodies, each perfect in its own and unique way, swinging around, displaying themselves. Suddenly Kim stopped in her tracks, stiffened up, hiccupped once, and fell over. Her eyes closed before she hit the arms that caught her.

"She's out cold," Chen said, lowering her to the floor and covering her with a robe draped over a nearby chair.

"Gurl can't hode her likor," Rona said, coming to a stop from her whirling-dervish dance of flying red hair. "Gib me anudder." She took the proffered drink, downed it in one swallow, smiled, and then she took a nosedive forward, falling into McCaughlin's wide arms. The big Scot placed her alongside her rival and covered her and the two began snoring, probably dreaming of one another as their heads lay so close together.

"Well, the weaker sex, I see, has fallen by the wayside," Panchali said. "And what of you, General Rockson, what are your drinking abilities? Are they beyond your beautiful concubines' abilities?"

"Load me up," Rock said with a corkscrew of a smile, "and we'll see what happens." They drank. And they drank some more. By 4:30 in the morning, there were but three men still conscious in the entire tent—Rockson, General Panchali, and Detroit. The trio sat around the table surrounded by bodies lying everywhere on the rug, snoring and groaning loudly. They had each drunk way, way too much exotic beverage but kept going, their eyes floating around inside their sockets like eggs looking for a frying pan.

"Now I'll get the *good* stuff," Panchali burped, stepping over the unconscious Ragdar, who had fallen long ago. He stumbled back a few seconds later with a small decanter that looked a thousand years old, poured each of them a glassful, and raised his own.

"To my whore of a mother and son-of-a-bitch of a father, who in their drunkenness, produced the greatest general the world has ever known." They swallowed the stuff and their gullets nearly exploded as the triple-distilled coconut-gin blasted into their stomach linings like a phosphorus bomb. Detroit's eyes rolled up like blinds on a spring and he tumbled backwards, out cold before he hit the ground.

"Looks lik 's jus' u 'n me now, Ger'l Rurkson," Panchali said, standing up. "Les shee wich un's the better man." Holding the bottle in one hand, he walked, lurching from side to side, and cleared a space, kicking bodies around him out of the way. "Ere, Rurkson, drink fer drink, punch fer punch—til

213

one man falls."

"Soun's like fun," Rock said, wiping his hand over his face, trying to focus the waves of color and darkness that spun around him like a flock of tumbling birds. He somehow made it over to Panchali, stepping over numerous fleshy piles, and stood in front of him, waving slowly from side to side as if a wind were blowing him.

"U first."

"No, I inshist," Rock replied with a smile. "Yur in my country and Ahm *yur* ghuest. Please." He put his hands behind his back and his chin out and closed his eyes. Panchali rolled up his long sleeves, wound up his right hand for about a minute, and then unleashed a powerhouse of a blow right into Rock's jaw. The Doomsday Warrior flew backward, crashing over tables, rolling over bodies, and not stopping until he reached the edge of the tent where he slammed into it. He shook his head hard as if someone had just dropped a bucket of marbles into it and, remembering vaguely where and who he was, rose unsteadily to his feet. Seeing Panchali staring at him, hands on hips, Rockson waved and headed over.

"Well, I'll be," Panchali said with real surprise. Not a man had ever risen from his punch before. Somewhere in the heart of his drunken being, Panchali suddenly felt a surge of warmth and respect for the Freefighter. For some men, like Panchali, must be bested by a man before they can truly be the other's friend. The general handed Rock another glassful of the nectar and they gulped it down.

"T'ink it's my twern," Rock said with an idiotic grin.

214

"Take your besh," Panchali muttered, closing his eyes and jutting his jaw in the middle of the air. Rockson pulled his fist back to his ear and shot it forward like a spear. The blow hit Panchali on the right side of his jaw and sent him twisting and tumbling through the air as if riding an invisible wave. He crashed through numerous objects, at last coming to rest halfway through a trough that had been up for drinking water.

Rockson waited nearly a minute, standing in one position, his body bending back and forth like a stalk of wheat, deciding whether or not to fall. Hearing nothing from his erstwhile opponent, he yelled over.

"P'nchaki, P'nchaki. I'm reddy fur the nex'." No one answered the request. "Well," the Doomsday Warrior said, looking around the floor full of drunken fighters, "guezz I won." With that he fell forward, his face landing dead center of a green silk pillow from which it didn't move for ten hours.

Chapter Sixteen

Colonel Killov strode the outer walkway of the twelfth floor of the Army Command building in the center of Fort Minsk. His was the highest position in the fortress city and from it he scanned the surrounding land with a pair of Super-scope Infrared binoculars. He knew they were coming. Vassily, Zhabnov—they couldn't just allow the KGB commander to take the whole thing over—not without a fight. Yet thus far . . . nothing. Killov was aware that they knew they would have to move soon or his hold over the entire Army apparatus would be complete. Already he had found out the location of five nuclear weapons and had taken possession of them. His plans were working out to a T. He was winning the Soviet power-struggle.

Yet within his churning guts acids of paranoia burned. For Killov had his own sixth sense—the intuition, the built-in warning system of the river rat. Far off to the east and south he could see some fires burning. But they were just primitively armed rabble, his recon scout had reported. A bunch of horsemen with swords, camping out in the open. If they *were* planning an attack, they would be hidden. Let them try. Killov laughed derisively into the wind. Yes, it would be amusing if those rag-tag mountain primitives tried to take this fort—with its twenty-foot-thick walls of concrete, its racks of heavy artillery and machine guns, auto-controlled and fired. Cannons against swords, tanks against horses. It would be amusing.

The Blackshirt commander reached inside his leather jacket and extracted a vial from which he took three Heighten-All's—a slightly hallucinogenic drug—for he wanted to add a bit of color to his vision. Just in case they came. Just in case the shells roared out red-and-blue and the bodies died like butchered dogs on the battlefield. He wanted to experience it all in psychedelic technicolor. He swallowed them down with a gulp from a small flask of vitamin-fortified vegetable juice—his one concession to his wasting flesh—and continued on his way around the wooden ramparts, which had been built in the early days of the fort as lookout towers. Though with the immense defensive capabilities of Minsk, they now seemed an anachronism, artifacts that had long since become obsolete.

Within minutes he could feel the mild psychedelic wash into his veins and fill him with a tingling sensation. His pupils began dilating, letting in more light to the chemical-saturated brain. The whole sky seemed to go by filled with galaxies of neon lights— like the ones in Moscow's Nevsky-Playa, or on the seamy side of Washington, D.C., where Pig Zhabnov had allowed the negros to run their honky-tonk joints and whorehouses, so he and his men could have their fun. Killov's mouth dropped open as the combined effects of the Heighten-All's mixed with the twenty other things he had taken that day, all reacting to make his blood feel like it was boiling, his veins as if electric currents were shooting through them. He felt — woozy.

He fell backward, landing against the cushioned outer wall of his dimly-lit suite of rooms. Feeling all his strength ooze out of him like sap, he slid down to the floor in a semi-daze. He shook his head, trying to come out of the mood, and then reached up and slapped himself hard ten times. Stars, galaxies, in a rush.

"There, that's better," the Blackshirt leader laughed. He could handle his drugs. Better than any goddamned man alive. Just needed a second or two to adjust. Now he felt wonderful, grand. His arteries swelled like the oceans, sending a tide of swooning sensations through his body. He slowly lifted the glasses again, barely moving, taking twenty seconds to bring them to his face. He tilted them up toward the flashing neon signs in the sky. The lights of the nebulas and star systems filled the glasses and poured into his maddened brain in a waterfall of images. He saw the actual meaning of his life.

"Incredible, incredible," the KGB master mumbled through lips as dried out as the back of an iguana standing on the equator. The stars filled him like messages from the dark gods at the far side of the universe. The glasses suddenly seemed to catch hold of an ultra-darkness, surrounded by swirling masses of burning diamonds. Killov tried to peer into it — into the void which called to him from a trillion light years off.

Yes, he could see—the magnetic circles of black flame pulling tighter and disappearing into a blackness that had no light. The drugs fully entered his system and in his hallucinations he was transported through the vast reaches of frozen space and into the spiraling darkness that burned deep with the star mass. He was moving in it now, part of it. And it was pure. Pure blackness. Without a trace of good or positive motion. Everything fell into it, everything went *down*. Down into the deepest of nowheres. Down into the dimension from which nothing— neither sun nor human soul—ever returns. And instinctively, Killov knew that this was his place of birth—his home. That he was a child of the blackness, that his flesh, his blood was made of that anti-matter, that anti-life. For he was entropy—in a human form. A super-concentrated manifestation of that energy which made things lose their life forces, run down, come apart at the seams. He—he was the Death Energy of the entire planet, meant to fall apart over billions of years—and now compressed into one man who would take it all with him. In a second. In a flash. The Earth. A nova of black fire in the galactic night. And Killov would accomplish what countless millions of years of erosion and decay, of atmospheric leakage and volcanic eruption, could not. The shattering of every atom on the planet earth—a destruction so complete that nothing would ever know it had been there.

In his madness, Colonel Killov, his mouth wide open with the stupefied drooling grin of an infant just fed at its mother's breast, joined with the darkest spectrums of the galactic night and charged himself with its destructive powers. For his food was nothing less than the atoms of pure evil of his own opium-driven dreams.

Rockson awoke with a groan and instantly wished he hadn't. The sound that was emitted through his jaws also jarred his skull, which throbbed as if a row of ice picks were being jabbed continuously in and out. He opened his eyes a millimeter at a time, trying not to wince from the light which sliced in, as that hurt, too. Where the hell was he? As his bloodshot orbs got to half mast, he saw the exotic designs on the wall-hangings across from him and then Detroit's sorry-looking face nursing a cup of hot coffee, his lips so deep into the hot steaming cup that his whole mouth seemed to disappear. The cup was lowered.

"Yo' bro'," Detroit whispered over from the table. "Have some coffee?" He pointed slowly with a trembling finger to another cup sitting next to him.

"What the hell—" Rock began and then winced again, his entire face sucking in like a prune from the exquisite pains that shot through him.

"Blood pressure, Rock, blood pressure," Detroit said as if he had just gone through it all himself. "Don't even *try* to think or say a word until you've had at least five cups of coffee—then we'll talk about it."

Heeding the advice, Rockson rose, taking one slow step at a time as if he were walking on rice paper, and deposited himself with a jarring thump in the chair next to the Freefighter. The coffee burned his lips but he could feel it cut through the drunken cobwebs in his skull instantly.

After the fourth sip, Rockson slowly surveyed the inside of the banquet tent. It was a wreck, as if a herd of elephants or at least water buffalo had thought it was the local wading pool and come to do some splashing. Everything in sight was cracked, broken, or crushed to a pulp. Trays of overturned food and bowls of squashed fruit lay in wild abandon of no particularly order or reason. Suddenly Rock realized that he and Detroit were the only ones in the place.

"Where the hell," he began again, rising up angrily in his seat, the blood shooting to his skull like the mercury in a thermometer when placed over an open flame. He came down again with a groan.

"I've been shot in the head and it's better than this," Rock said, turning and looking at Detroit, eyes tearing slightly. "But where, may I ask," Rock said as softly and calmly as he could, "is everyone else?"

"Gone, Rock," Detroit answered, reaching for another cup of black liquid.

"What the hell—?" By now the Pavlovian response of being rewarded with pain made Rock stop voluntarily as he mouthed the third word—but it was too late as another wall of little razor blades slammed down on the softest part of his brain tissue. Twenty seconds later, he asked again, this time in a whisper.

"Tell me, pray tell—where did they go?"

"To the battle site, Rock—but cool down, pal," Detroit said, holding his hand up, "we got plenty of time. You and me—we drank that blue stuff. That's why we're here—and everyone else split. Stuff's *strong*, Rock. My head feels like it fell into the receiving basket for a guillotine."

"If they start that battle without me I'll kill the bastards," Rock said between clenched teeth, trying to fool his blood pressure. He didn't. Detroit told Rock that Rona and Kim were sleeping it off in the next tent. Rock stole a peek, and was satisfied.

Half an hour later, both men headed haltingly outside and found their 'brids tied to a post. There was still activity in the Sikh camp, men manning kitchens and command tents—but clearly the bulk of the army was gone. They rode through the woods, going eight miles out of the way to reach the northern approach to Minsk. Here the going got really rough as the ground became cratered with sharp, cutting coral-like rock formations that even the 'brids, with their thick shoes and hooves, had a hard time maneuvering. Slowly Rock's headache vanished as he stretched out his arms and legs, twisting the muscles this way and that while he rode, trying to work them free of a thousand kinks.

Rona was the first to stir. She sat up sharply. "Where am I?—Oh!" She remembered the near-naked dance she had done with—"Kim!" she shouted, shaking the blonde lying next to her awake. "Hurry up—we're going to miss the battle!"

Kim moaned and sat up. She focused her eyes on the redhead who continued. "Hurry! We need some clothes."

They looked around, found their combat fatigues and liberator rifles on an oak chest.

While they dressed, Rona said, "Kim, we—one of

223

us might die out there today—I think—"

"Yeah," Kim smiled. "Let's shake on it. If we live, we'll work something out—about Rock. I've grown fond of you—" She bit her lip.

"And I of you, Kim. Let's be friends—"

With a handshake, they declared a personal truce, then left the tent.

By the time he and Detroit reached Panchali's and Ragdar's forces hidden in woods a half mile from the northern reach, the sun was setting fast and Rock's guts were finally sorting themselves out.

"Ah, General Rockson," Panchali said with a broad grin as the Doomsday Warrior rode up and dismounted. "We wondered if you were going to make it at all."

"I better not find out you put poison or something in that juice you were feeding me last night," Rock said as he looked around at the Sikh forces which spread far back into the woods, taking in the rows of archers, horsemen, and the immense devices that the generals had built

"Come now, General Rockson, we have much to do," Panchali said with a smile, putting his arm around the Freefighter's shoulder. Having beaten him in drinking and punch-me-punch-you, he was, as far as the Sikh was concerned, an honorary member of the Royal Sikh Army. "Come, see our siege equipment," Panchali said with pride as he led Rockson to a grove of high trees beneath which sat ten immense wooden contraptions, apparently pulled by hand all the way around the fort. Rockson walked up to the exotic war machines, staring at the wide wheels, the steel cups at the ends of the long wooden poles which were attached to pieces of rubber stretched far back, ready to snap their loads forward.

"Catapults, General Rockson," Sikh Ragdar said, jumping down from the platform of one where he was supervising final adjustments on the ancient device. "A weapon as old as war itself," the young Asian general declared, walking over to Rockson and Panchali. "But as you'll see, effective — yes, quite effective." The air of confidence that both generals possessed unnerved Rockson, since he didn't know whether they could really do everything they claimed or were actually madmen carrying out a terrible bluff that would bring him and his men into the jaws of catastrophe.

"This — this is your artillery?" Rockson asked with growing trepidation, his head threatening to start pounding again at any moment.

"This and our artillery units, of course," Panchali said, sweeping his hand to the right where hundreds of men sat cross-legged, their long bows next to them, quivers of arrows behind their backs awaiting the call to attack.

Rockson put his hand over his face, feeling slightly faint, and groaned. "Giant slingshots and bows and arrows — that's how we're going to take on Killov? Just blow and the walls come tumbling down?"

"Exactly, General Rockson," Panchali said, slapping him hard on the back. "We'll huff and we'll puff and we'll blow those goddamned walls straight down to hell."

Chapter Seventeen

All across America, in the dead of the night, the Freefighters and their Sikh allies edged toward the KGB-controlled Red fortresses. Catapult and machine gun, mortar and grenade units—all marched side by side toward the imposing walls of the concrete cities looking skeptically at one another—as if scarcely daring to believe that they were on the same side of the war together. But love and death make strange bedfellows—and what man will dare tell the man covering his flank to go, leaving him exposed? So they shut their mouths and marched and tried to guess—since men are wont to die when they march into battle—just who would be alive and who dead when the morning sun cast a crying eye on the bloody fields of dawn. At the stroke of 1:00 A.M. they struck. K-Day, Killov's day to die, had arrived.

All was bedlam in the woods north of Fort Minsk as the Sikh army made its final preparations. The immense catapults, looking more like mobile draw-bridges than functioning weapons, were pushed up to the very edges of the forest and placed in open spaces between groves of trees so they had a clear line of fire to the fortress. Other towering devices made of logs lashed together in upright configurations were also placed near the mile-long clearing that surrounded the Red stronghold. But Rock, sitting on the sidelines, couldn't figure out what the hell they were—as he saw no buckets for heaving things, no stretched strips of rubber pulling their load back. He and the Rock team—Archer, Chen, McCaughlin, Detroit—stood by the edge of the woods watching Panchali and Ragdar rush madly around on horseback overseeing the last-second adjustments and problems. The Freefighters had never felt so helpless. *They* were the ones who strode into battle in the first ranks, the men who were used to running shows, not being stagehands in them. They sat on their haunches resting for the battle and watched what may have been—next to them—pound for pound the toughest fighting force on earth.

"Catapult crews—man your weapons," Panchali screamed out through cupped hands from atop his Arabian stallion. Robed, turbaned warriors rushed to the weapons and filled their yard-wide steel cups with wooden boxes sealed tight as drums, packing two or three of them into each firing cup.

"First inning," Rock said as he and the others stood up, unslinging their Liberators, Chen his starknives, Archer his sturdy crossbow. The Doomsday Warrior looked over to the left about 150 yards away where half of the Century City Freefighter army milled about, waiting for their chance. The rest of the men were spread around Fort Minsk to create diversionary attacks against the other three walls. The fortress looked impregnable from where Rockson stood, a veritable mountain taking up the whole sky to the north. He felt a churning sickly feeling in his stomach as he wondered if his whole plan to ally with the Reds was insane, if he'd perhaps gone mad from breathing in too many radioactive poisons.

"Fire!" Panchali screamed, whipping his long curved scimitar through the air in a lightning flash. The "artillery" units slammed long metal levers on the sides of the catapults and the tree-sized arms shot up and forward, pulled by the super-taut, foot-thick plasti/rubber slings. The loads shot like rockets through the night air, the boxes spinning wildly, end over end, with none of the perfect trajectories or geometric purity associated with the smooth arc of an artillery shell. But then beauty doesn't matter much when you're trying to blow the other man into mush. Nearly twenty of the explosive-filled crates migrated over the barren field in a curve that took them almost 300 feet up. They reached their peak altitude just about mid-field and then came barreling down like a shipment of supermarket goods lost in space.

Several of the guards patrolling the twenty-foot wide walkway atop the north wall had a few seconds to rub their eyes and wonder if they'd been drinking too much as they saw the sky raining boxes. Just a few seconds. Then the TNT-laden parcels slammed into the top and side of the wall and released their pent-up energy in a fraction of a second. Tremendous explosions lit the night, making the entire field between the Freefighters and the fort as bright as day for a moment as the special deliveries ripped out boulder-sized chunks from the wall and sent them whirling off along with clouds of concrete dust. The catapult teams instantly pulled the firing cups back down, winding them back on a pulley, and loaded them up with more "Dust Makers," as they were known to the Sikhs who manned them.

"Fire!" Panchali screamed out again, bringing his sword down as if he were slicking off a head. Another load of careening crates took off with all the grace of a one-legged orangutan. But somehow, though they flew completely lopsided, looking as if they should just drop from the sky like stones, they bee-lined toward their targets, every one coming down within thirty feet of their targets. The north wall of Fort Minsk shook as if in the grip of an earthquake as hairline fractures spider-webbed across it and more truck-sized chunks were bitten out from the top and spat into a dusty cloud that rose into the night air.

"Fire at will," Panchali commanded the catapulters, who began sending off a barrage every thirty seconds. The Sikh general turned to a second line of warriors, standing behind the high wooden walls that had been constructed.

"Shields forward," Panchali yelled, spinning his sword around above his head like a propeller blade. "Archers forward!" Eight of the sixty-foot-high wooden constructions, built on wheels as tall as two men, started forward, each hauled by a team of a dozen horses. They moved slowly, creaking as if they would topple over, but they moved—out of the woods and across the field toward the fortress already lit up with curtains of flame where some of the explosives cases had ignited wooden structures just inside.

Teams of archers, their quivers bursting with arrows mounted with sticks of dynamite, marched behind each of the moving walls of lashed trees and branches, their bows filled and ready.

"When the hell do *we* get to join the party?" Detroit yelled out to Ragdar who rode over to the mounted Freefighters, champing at the bit to get into the action.

"Ah, first we must soften up the meat, tenderize it," Ragdar laughed, showing a mouthful of pearly teeth. "Then we will eat the beast." He laughed again and headed off to give final orders to the next assault force that had moved up from the woods to the edge of the open fields—thousands of Sikhs carrying long wooden ladders beneath their arms—twenty men to a ladder, kneeling in the dirt as they awaited the go-ahead order.

The giant wooden shields had gotten only halfway to the fort when the batteries atop the north wall which hadn't yet been damaged opened up from every side. Flares shot up from the KGB gunners and burst into light, illuminating the cleared field with the intensity of a noonday sun. But a stream of arrows instantly shot into the air from behind the moving walls, zeroing in on the flares. They detonated with loud pops high above the Sikh archers' heads—and took out the burning flares, disintegrating them with the blast force.

Detroit whistled through his teeth as he sat atop his 'brid next to Rockson. "These fucking guys got their shit together," the black Freefighter said appreciatively. "And I thought I knew it all. See that?"

"It's what you could call the crude approach to

war," Chen said. "Just blow up everything in your way."

"Crude, but efficient," Rock answered. "Frighteningly efficient." They watched as the archers, protected from exploding artillery shrapnel by the fort, drew to within a hundred yards of the wall. Suddenly they rushed from behind the mobile shields and unleashed a volley of arrows over the top of the shattered ramparts. The dynamite-laden barbs filled the air like a swarm of locusts, looking for a field of vegetation. They descended on the other side and hundreds of small explosions could be heard all the way across the field. The moment one group had released their arrows they ran back behind the wooden wall and another squad rushed out to release their own deadly volley. Hundreds, thousands of the arrows filled the sky, wreaking havoc wherever they landed. Cannons and machine-gun emplacements, along with the KGB'ers lining the walls, were blown into bloody rubble as the fusillade of high explosives coming in like bullets exacted a terrible toll.

"Ladder squads forward," Panchali commanded, riding amongst the infantry and main part of the Sikh force, urging them on, giving them his mad energy to kill, infusing them with his fighting spirit. Thousands of Sikh warriors streamed out across the field at full run, holding the long rickety ladders beneath their arms. They let out a shrill war cry as they ran that sent shivers up even the Freefighters' spines. A sound of primordial challenge, an ear-splitting melody that sang out the pre-eminence of death. When the ladder men had reached mid-field, Panchali turned to Rockson and with a smile, said

232

simply:

"Now, it is *our* turn." He raised his sword as Rock leaned around and gave his own hand signal to his troops to move. They started forward slowly at first, Rock and his men—and women—right alongside Panchali and Ragdar, their mounts chafing at the bit from standing around for hours. From out of the woods along a five-hundred-yard front, the horsemen emerged—the Sikh fighters carrying brilliantly colored war banners, their swords pulled free of jeweled scabbards. And across the field from them, their handguns and 9mm Liberators in their hands, the Freefighters in their olive and khaki combat uniforms.

"Toward the center wall there," Panchali screamed out to Rockson above the roar of the battle. "Where it's been most damaged." The Sikh general pointed the way with the tip of his gleaming sword, curved like the backbone of a cobra about to strike. The Doomsday Warrior squinted through the mist of cordite and powdered dirt and saw that the crates had done their work. Dead center of the mile-long wall, still shrouded in dust, a hole had been blown right through—rubble-filled but passable.

They were about halfway to their destination when the remaining artillery units on the wall opened up on the charging cavalry, at last having a target they could sight. Hundreds of the horsemen and their steeds went flying into the air as shells tore into their midst. Arms, legs, and heads flew indiscriminately in all directions. But the commando squads reached the wall at that very moment and as the catapults far behind stopped their barrage, the Sikh fighters threw the rickety assault ladders up against the walls and shot up them like cats climbing trees. Within seconds they were over the top and engaging in fierce hand-to-hand fighting with the confused KGB troops on the ramparts. But trembling Turganev revolvers are no match for swinging swords cutting off limbs like human scythes, and the advance units took out much of the north wall artillery crew within seconds. They swept up and down the wide walkway, out toward the other walls, which continued to fire at the diversionary attacks from the other three sides.

As the cavalry came to within a hundred yards of Minsk, bodies of fallen Sikhs filled the ground and the steeds had to stomp through them, grinding the flesh beneath their hooves into red mud. The break in the wall appeared larger as they flew toward it and Rock pulled out his .12 gauge death dealer, leaning forward on Snorter's back to make himself less of a target.

"We kill or we die," Panchali yelled to Rockson as he guided his stallion at full gallop toward the opening. His sword, held high above his ruby-laden turban, looked like the shimmering lightning bolt of a god, ready to descend and take out whole cities.

Rock and the Sikh general were the first to reach the wall and they pushed their steeds up and over the smoking pile of rubble that had once been the impenetrable north side of Fort Minsk. The animals slipped and stumbled on the piled chunks of mortar and steel but made it up to the top of the heap, rising a good fifteen feet from the ground, and headed down the other side right into the belly of the beast. And smack into a welcoming committee of heavily armed KGB troops who had pulled back to a second defensive perimeter inside the walled fort. The leaders of the Sikh and Freefighting forces rode into the enemy full speed, sending bodies flying from the charging mass of their mounts. Rockson fired his shotpistol continuously, whipping it around, while Panchali used only his sword, slashing in every direction, causing whole heads to depart their bodies as if they'd been launched from them. The KGB'ers tried to bring down the riders by firing at them, trying to grab at them as they swarmed over the invaders like ants. But there were just too many and they shot through the crowd, dispatching Blackshirts to the grave by the dozen.

It was a bloodbath. The red liquid spurted from hacked bodies and formed widening puddles. In an ordinary fight the KGB troops, who were tough, hardened fighters in their own right, would have made a go of it. But the war-screams of the Sikh warriors, the slashing swords, the heads of their comrades flying by them, and the cyclone of Freefighters firing as fast as their fingers could pull their triggers unnerved them. It was as if they were facing super-soldiers, men without a flicker of fear in their blood-hungry eyes. It was that hesitation, the knowledge that they were doomed to defeat that marked them as beaten from the start. And beaten men are sitting targets for those filled with the will to destroy.

Rockson glanced over at Panchali as the two of them pushed their mounts through the disorganized resistance. The man looked more than human, his jeweled robe swirling through the air, reflecting the myriad small fires around them like a cloak of electric sparks. The Sikh general's eyes were wide as saucers, his expression vicious and unforgiving as his sword hand came down again and again like a machine. For a split second, Rockson remembered an ancient Hindu painting he had seen in a dusty book, a picture of Siva, the God of Destruction, wading through an army with just such a sword. No wonder the KGB troops ran in terror, facing such a demon. For Panchali existed to kill, his face alive and filled with fury, his eyes darting like a hawk's from side to side while slicing every offending arm, every proffered rifle in two. He looked for the life of him as if he were in paradise, dancing the waltz of destruction with the fiery angels.

The Doomsday Warrior suddenly felt a shape coming at him from the right and turned to see three KGB'ers kneeling on a ten-foot-high wall, sighting him up. He pulled the trigger of his .12 gauge, knowing as the heavy weapon bucked in his hand that he couldn't get all three. His stomach clenched involuntarily as he waited to receive the return fire. The teflon-coated steel pellets from his shell slammed into the chest of the attacker on the right, grinding bone and lung into instant pudding. But as the two others got Rockson fitted in their sights and went for the triggers, a mini-buzzsaw came whirling from the clouds of dust and slammed into the cinder blocks at their feet. Both were blown apart at the thighs, their legs falling down in shapeless red masses to the ground below while the rest of them shot into the air and came down behind the wall, ready-fitted for coffins.

Rockson turned and saw Chen, galloping about fifty feet off, raise his arm for a split second and Rockson returned the salute. Then the Chinese had his own business to attend to, as two black-suited figures tried to grab him from each side of his 'brid. Rock knew that the man could take care of himself — he'd have to — and glanced around quickly, seeing the rest of his team and even Rona and Kim, right in the thick of it, riding side by side, sending out a blistering wall of firepower that blasted everything in front of them as they went. McCaughlin had somehow tied the .50 cal. smg to the top of his stout 'brid and was firing the thing right over the animal's head, having been thoughtful enough to place a pillow of thick cloth between the smoking machine gun and the creature's skull.

Rock and Panchali shot ahead suddenly, seeing an opening, as dozens of the KGB defenders were blasted aside from two of Detroit's grenades. They were through the gap before the smoke had cleared or the pieces of steaming humanity had fallen from the air in a snowstorm of flesh.

Rock slammed another clip into his .12 gauger as they galloped into a long wide corridor with rounded walls and ceilings made of thousands of hand-painted ceramic tiles. The slamming hooves of their mounts echoed like drumbeats off the shining walls. On the other side was a wide square and more streaming units of KGB all heading to the north wall. But in their terrified faces Rockson could already see the seeds of defeat. They didn't know what was happening or how to respond to it. The two mounted figures roared through the ranks like express trains, coming at them with such speed the men couldn't even raise their rifles to fire. Again Panchali's sword rose and fell, like the judging arm of fate itself, finding a skull, a throat, a chest at every descent. Rock's hand bounced around as he held tight to the bucking shotpistol that spat out its loads in loud cracks of smoke, the shells automatically ejecting and flying up past him as he rode. At such close range, firing into faces just feet away, the destructive power of the handgun was magnified ten-fold. Whole skulls split apart, leaving headless corpses to topple over at their leisure. Spinal columns shattered right out of the backs of black leather jackets, bent and twisted like the spokes of a broken bicycle wheel dipped in red. They came—they saw—and they left behind a field of corpses plowed into their own blood. What the KGB had sowed they would now reap—and the crop would be their own destruction.

Suddenly the two men were past the troops and in a large oval intersection from which all the roads of the city seemed to fan out. They pulled their steeds to a stop for a moment as Rockson looked around, trying to determine the right direction. Everywhere the sounds of fighting, of bullets whizzing, of dynamite erupting in cratered roars, the screams and war cries of the combatants all filled the air with the deafening cacophony of battle.

"I love it," General Panchali said, turning to Rockson with a wild look in his eyes. His sword and white robe were now saturated with blood as if they'd been dyed that color. His jewels peeked through the coating of human flesh, sending out an occasional sliver of light. "I can't deny it, Rockson," the silver-bearded

238

Sikh warrior laughed, holding his sword to the skies. "I love every damned minute of it. I haven't felt so alive for months."

"You look like you're enjoying yourself," the Doomsday Warrior shouted above the din of battle, as he at last sighted the Russian street sign pointing the way to the Command Center.

"Where to now, Freefighter?" the Sikh general asked with a glow in his eyes, wanting to wade into the human ranks again.

"I'm gonna get that bastard Killov," Rock said, taking another clip of shells and putting it in his rein hand so he could reload on the run. "He's the key. With him captured—or dead, the coup will fall apart throughout America. But it's going to be bad in there," he warned, pointing with his pistol hand to the center of the fortress city. "Killov will have his elite forces surrounding the building. The first ones in there are going to be met by an army. Maybe you should—"

"Trying to keep all the fun to yourself, Freefighter," Panchali said with a bark. "Lead on, General Rockson. I have not yet begun to kill."

Chapter Eighteen

They galloped neck and neck like racehorses trying to beat each other to the finish, down the widest boulevard of Fort Minsk—Trotsky Avenue—toward the Command building which rose from the center of the now smoke-enshrouded city. Two blocks ahead Rockson saw the sandbagged emplacements of the KGB commander's elite forces, ready to give their lives to save Killov's. The machine-gun squads saw the riders as well and opened up from ten different positions, sending a blizzard of .50 caliber slugs whistling down the avenue. But Rock pulled Snorter's reins sharply to the right, making the hybrid wheel about and push Panchali's horse along with it. Both steeds flew down a side street, nearly losing their balance from the sudden turn, but within a few strides gained it again.

"We'll have to come in from the rear," Rockson screamed out as a series of secondary blasts shook the ground beneath their feet as one of the fortress's munitions depots went up with the explosive power of a small A-bomb. "They're too well fortified up front." They made their way down the narrow streets, heading all the way around the twelve-story central head-quarters.

Suddenly from out of nowhere a KGB'er jumped forward, firing his rifle and stabbing forward with the eighteen-inch-long bayonet mounted on the barrel. The bullet missing Panchali who was nearer the attacker, but the knife blade caught him in mid-thigh, sending him flying off the back of the stallion and onto the street. As he hit the unevenly paved road, the Sikh general sliced behind his head with the sword, ripping across the KGB'er's stomach. Whatever plans the Blackshirt had had for dispatching the Sikh fighter vanished as his belly spewed out in a gush of red.

Rock pulled his 'brid to a stop and turned to see dozens of the black jackets pouring from a doorway toward the fallen Sikh.

"Go ahead, leave me," Panchali shouted, preparing to swing the sword and pulling out the snub-nosed .44 mag pistol from beneath his robe.

"Right," the Doomsday Warrior spat out from the side of his mouth as he kicked Snorter and shot into the wall of KGB elite troops who had closed in on the fallen warrior. But they had bitten off more than they could chew as Rockson and the Sikh went wild, both of them sighting and firing, slashing, kicking out like whirlwinds of death. Within seconds half of the attacking Blackshirts were lying on the ground, dead or wishing they were as their severed arteries vomited out every drop within. As Rock's .12 gauge shotpistol clicked empty he jumped down from his 'brid and pulled out his long-bladed hunting knife, courtesy of the Sioux nation, and dove into the thick of it—a blur of muscle and an impossible catch, ripping at every shape he saw.

Before they knew it, it was over. The two of them stood back to back, their heads snapping around like owls, searching out the next man who wanted to die. But there were no more takers. The three KGB who were left pulled back, looked down at the remains of their comrades, and turned, throwing their weapons down as they disappeared into a dark basement to hide.

"I told you to keep going," Panchali shouted to Rockson as they remounted.

"Disobeyed orders," Rock grinned. "You'll have to courtmartial me when it's over." Panchali gave a flash of a smile of thanks to the Doomsday Warrior, but in his soldier's heart he felt wounded, not wishing to owe his life to any man. The Sikh ripped one of the silk scarves from his neck and tied it around his leg to stop the flow of blood.

"Can you ride?" Rock asked.

"My corpse could handle a horse better than most living men," Panchali snapped back and the two warriors shot forward again, their steeds jumping over the odd assortment of bodies and appendages on the street. They rode for another five blocks and came up behind the building. But again it was as well guarded as the front and they had to pull back quickly, ducking behind a building wall to escape the hail of slugs.

"This ain't gonna work," Rock said, dismounting. "We can't come in head-on—we'll have to sneak in."

"Never," Panchali said, sitting stubbornly atop his stallion. "A Sikh warrior must attack his enemy head-on, or—"

"Or bullshit," Rock said, his voice rising. "If you want to donate your body to the butcher's heap, be my guest. But I'm more interested in ending this whole damned thing. There'll be other wars, pal. Other charges with bugles blowing." He turned and started toward a smaller building that faced the Command Center without waiting to see if the Asian general was going to follow.

As he came to a locked door and put his shoulder against it, Rock felt the Sikh's presence just behind him.

"All right, all right, we'll do it your way," Panchali muttered into his ear. "But how the hell are we going to get in there, anyway?"

"The Reds often build underground tunnels linking their various command buildings—just in case of attack. But we can use them for our purposes as well—*for* attack." Rock pulled back a few inches and then slammed forward with all his mutant strength, snapping the lock on the inside. The steel door flew open and the two fighters par excellence rushed through, weapons at the ready, but the dimly lit underground passage was unguarded, at least at this end. With Rockson in the lead they ran along the crumbling corridor, much in need of repair as the Reds apparently hadn't paid attention to it for years. Doors stood half open on both sides of them, falling half off their hinges—and inside were darkened storage rooms, filled with the scent of rot and decay. Though there were numerous leadoffs heading in all directions, Rock steered them straight on toward where he figured the Command Building to be.

Sure enough, they came to the end of the main tunnel and then up some stairs to another locked door. On the other side they could hear voices mumbling in frantic Russian about just what the hell was going on out there as the explosions and the gunfire were growing closer by the minute. Rock and Panchali stood facing each other on the top step and at a nod from the Doomsday Warrior, they both slammed their shoulders against the structure and burst through. They found themselves, when they had risen from the floor, in the center of a machine-gun nest — bad luck for the opposition as the tripod-mounted .50 caliber smg was pointed in the other direction, toward the main front doors. Before the five KGB'ers could find their handguns, Panchali's sword had found two necks to dissect and Rock's fist two faces that shattered beneath his knuckles like leftovers in a bowl of cherry pie mix. The fifth KGB trooper made the mistake of pulling his knife and waving it in Panchali's face instead of running. The Sikh general made a grimace of disgust at such a feeble gesture, slicing the knife and the hand holding it clear off the man's body in one swing, and with the backward stroke nearly cleaved the man in two at the waist, the messy sack that was left of him tumbling over to join his fighting buddies in their long sleep.

Now that Panchali was killing again he seemed to get a little less disgruntled, the semblance of a pleased expression returning to his stony face.

"Come on," Rockson yelled as he heard a squad's worth of boots slamming down on the corridor floor just around the corner. "These are the peons — we're after El Excellente himself."

He searched frantically around the wide floor and saw it—the elevator bank. Grabbing Panchali by the sleeve, Rock rushed over and pressed the "up" button on all four panels. A heavy whir of grinding gears and whining cables issued forth and the green light above one lit up as the door slid open. They virtually flew inside, slamming into the back wall as the elevator was much smaller than he had thought. Rock turned and found the buttons and instinctively punched 12—the top floor—sensing in his gut that Killov, with his eightieth-floor suite back at his command center in the Monolith in Denver, Colorado, would have chosen the highest vantage point here as well.

His finger had barely pressed the button when heavily armed KGB commandos came storming around the hall and sighted the two intruders. They lifted their smg's and unleashed a storm that would have cut an elephant in two. But the doors slammed shut with a satisfying bang and the elevator headed upstairs as Rock and Panchali heard the pinging of countless slugs against the steel doors below.

"This is it, General," Rock said as the "10" and then the "11" flashed on the indicator board. "When we hit '12'—move as fast as you've ever moved in your life. This—this Killov is no ordinary man."

"No—?" Panchali asked with a curious expression. "How interesting. I'm growing bored with killing ordinary men—it's like shooting carp in a pond. Perhaps we will have a worthy challenge." Rockson threw a skeptical look at Panchali but didn't have time to debate the man's character as "12" lit up and the doors flew open.

It wasn't that Panchali was slow, but that Rockson was just a millimeter faster. He saw the five men standing yards from the doors, their rifles aimed dead forward, and reacted with the speed of a striking piranha. As he dove forward, Rock kicked Panchali's leg out from under him, bringing the man down like a stone to the corridor floor. The KGB assassins opened up like a firing squad, sure they had the men in their graves. But the slugs only found closing elevator doors and ricocheted off, careening backwards. Rockson's .12 gauge equalizer was in his hands at the moment the Reds fired. By the time they realized they'd missed, his finger had moved three times. Five bodies flew backward as if hit by the fist of God himself, leaving five bright red trails on the floor all the way to the back wall, fifteen feet behind them.

"That's the second time, Freefighter," Panchali said, jumping to his feet, "that you've saved my life. I am growing too indebted to you."

"Forget it, man," Rock said as they headed down the hall on their toes. "Just your coming to this country, where every goddamned thing seems to want to kill a man or at least take a bite out of him, is payment a thousand times over."

As they went down the hall they kicked open doors, ready to incinerate whatever was inside. But all the rooms were empty. They came to the last and main door at the end of the corridor and again, facing each other just inches apart, shoulder-slammed into it, smashing the rectangle from its hinges. Both men stumbled into the room, their weapons high.

"Ah, welcome, gentlemen," said a cold voice dripping with lies and deceit in every word. "I've been expecting you. Although I didn't realize I was going to have two guests." Both fighters focused on the man who sat in the misty dimness at the far end of the room behind a long wooden desk, both hands clasped together on the heavily waxed top. Could it be — *him*? Killov?

"Thanks for the greeting," Rockson said, his shot-pistol pointed at the calm man's chest, as he and the Sikh walked forward.

The gaunt man's face moved out of the shadows. Rockson would know it anywhere. The evil skull features, the reddish scar he had himself placed on that face-of-death. *"Killov!"* Rockson snarled. "You are our prisoner, you will stand trial for war crimes — or die right here, right now. However you want it, *bastard*."

"Tsk, tsk," Killov said, his eyes wide, the pupils dilated big as quarters. "You really should be taught some manners. Pity you won't get the chance to learn." Still his long pale hands were plainly in sight. Rockson didn't get his making threats.

"You must finally be cracking, slime, from all those drugs you pile into that skeleton of a body," Rockson sneered. "I think you're the one who's finished — not us."

"Perhaps there are factors you don't know about," the KGB commander said with the icy smoothness of a razor cutting flesh.

"Like what?" Rockson asked, his eyes darting suddenly around the room, searching for hidden attackers.

"Like this!" Killov screamed, all the rage he had

248

been suppressing over the imminent loss of Minsk exploding from him. The Blackshirt leader pushed his knee up hard under the desk and thus pressed a button. Whether he was intending to reach Killov with his sword, or to shield Rockson from what was coming, the Doomsday Warrior couldn't tell—but suddenly Panchali was jumping in front of him. There was as roar from the whole front side of Killov's desk as the wooden panels flew off and a mounted rack of ten arrayed shotguns fired simultaneously at waist level. The wall of shots hit the Sikh general dead on, ripping into every part of his torso. Rockson, standing three feet behind him, was shielded from the majority of the blasts though he felt stabbing pellet fragments rip into his right shoulder and leg. Panchali was thrown straight backward as if running in reverse and slammed into Rockson, dropping them both down. Before he even made contact with the floor, Rock had his pistol up and pulled the trigger over and over again until the chamber was empty.

But before a single one of his shells could take root in the mad KGBer's flesh, Killov had already pushed another button. A peeled-open steel globe shot up from the floor and snapped closed around his entire chair, shielding the madman inside in an impenetrable cocoon. Rock's shots bounced harmlessly off the thick outer alloy-layering. Suddenly the room was filled with a deep vibration and a rocket system ignited on the underside of the diving-bell shaped device.

Using all his strength, Rockson pulled the dead weight of Panchali out of the way of the flames emerging from the desk as the heat swept by them both like the fire of a furnace. The white ignition flame changed to the blast of a full-sized escape-rocket taking off and the globe shot backward, smashing right through the twelfth-floor wall and out into the air.

Rockson ran forward and coughing from the hot smoke, peered through the twisted opening, pieces of wall still tumbling to the street below, and saw the escape device shooting through the night like a meteor until it disappeared far over the vast woods to the north of them. Rock let his gaze fall to the streets below where Freefighters and Sikhs were streaming past the Command Building. The KGB was in full retreat now, many of them driving vehicles at full speed trying to get out the back entrance of the fort. But there would be no escape for them. Only their master had made it out.

Rock walked back to Panchali and knelt down beside him. The man was still alive, his eyes open and weakly alert. But the Doomsday Warrior had been around too many wounded, too many dying not to know that the Sikh didn't have a chance. He was bleeding in over thirty places, thick streams of red that pulsed, and emptied out his life onto the floor around him. Rock reached down and put one arm under the man's head, lifting him slightly so he could breathe easier.

"Thank you, Freefighter," Panchali said as he looked up at Rockson with a smug smile. "See—I repaid you. Now we are even."

"No—now I am once again in your debt," Rock said softly. "And I don't know if I'm going to get the chance to repay you," he whispered so low it could hardly be heard.

"Don't whimper like a raw recruit," Panchali barked out, coughing up blood. "I know I'm dying. It is obvious. But Rockson," he said, looking the Doomsday Warrior square in the eye, with incredible power in his gaze even as he lay mortally wounded, "do not mourn for me. My life has been a miraculous adventure — and my greatest wish in life — to die in the midst of glorious foreign battle — has been granted. Can you see me growing old and fat, sitting at a desk? No! I go now on the river of my own blood across the Styx into the land of fallen warriors." He held his hand out and squeezed it tightly around Rockson's. "I shall see you there someday — friend." His hand tightened and then relaxed and Rockson knew — it was over.